P9-DYD-379

F
DOG

cop. 1

A Dog's life

F
DOG

A Dog's life

cop. 1

DATE	BORROWER'S NAME
	Michele 23
	Rosalyn 23

© THE BAKER & TAYLOR CO.

A Dog's Life
Stories of Champions, Hunters, and Faithful Friends

Other Collections by Phyllis R. Fenner

A Dog's Life
Stories of Champions, Hunters, and Faithful Friends

Selected by Phyllis R. Fenner
Illustrated by Lloyd Bloom

William Morrow and Company
New York   1978

Library of Congress Cataloging in Publication Data

A Dog's life.   Summary: A collection of short stories about one of man's favorite companions—the dog. 1. Dogs—Legends and stories. 2. Short stories, American. [1. Dogs—Fiction.   2. Short stories] I. Fenner, Phyllis Reid (date) II. Bloom, Lloyd. PZ10.3.D7107   [Fic]   78-6580 ISBN 0-688-22156-4   ISBN 0-688-32156-9 lib. bdg.

Printed in the United States of America.
First Edition
1   2   3   4   5   6   7   8   9   10

I fell in love with an
Irish setter.
This book is in memory of
Scooter.

Contents

The Best Kind of Dog

What is the best kind of dog to own? The kind you have! Big or little, long-haired or short, it doesn't matter. Although dogs can be possessive and jealous, their hearts are big, their minds keen, and their loyalty unquestioned. They ask little and give much.

The dog has been man's companion for more than ten thousand years, not only hunting with him and guarding his home, but as a pet, too. Pictures of hunters and their dogs are on the walls of Spanish caves; dog figures are on Egyptian tombs and Assyrian tablets; hunters and dogs are depicted in early Chinese paintings, and the Greeks and

Romans told stories about dogs. Today we are a nation of dog owners. There are more than twenty-five million dogs in the United States; five million puppies are born each year.

Someone said that it is a comfort to the man who makes a fool of himself over a dog to know that the dog makes just as big a fool of himself over the man. This book is a tribute to all dogs and to those enslaved by them.

P.F.

Weep No More, My Lady

James Street

The moonlight symphony of swamp creatures hushed abruptly, and the dismal bog was peaceful as unborn time and seemed to brood in its silence. The gaunt man glanced back at the boy and motioned for him to be quiet, but it was too late. Their presence was discovered. A jumbo frog rumbled a warning and the swamp squirmed into life as its denizens scuttled to safety.

Fox fire was glowing to the west and the bayou was slapping the cypress knees when suddenly a haunting laugh echoed through the wilderness, a strange chuckling yodel ending in a weird *gro-o-o.*

The boy's eyes were wide and staring. "That's it, Uncle Jess. Come on! Let's catch it!"

"Uh, oh." The man gripped his shotgun. "That ain't no animal. That's a thing."

They hurried noiselessly in the direction of the sound that Skeeter had been hearing for several nights. Swamp born and reared, they feared nothing they could shoot or outwit, so they slipped out of the morass and to the side of a ridge. Suddenly Jesse put out his hand and stopped the child, then pointed up the slope. The animal, clearly visible in the moonlight, was sitting on its haunches, its head cocked sideways as it chuckled. It was a merry and rather melodious little chuckle.

Skeeter grinned in spite of his surprise, then said, "Sh-h-h. It'll smell us."

Jesse said, "Can't nothing smell that far. Wonder what the durn thing is?" He peered up the ridge, studying the creature. He had no intention of shooting unless attacked, for Jesse Tolliver and his nephew never killed wantonly.

The animal, however, did smell them and whipped her nose into the wind, crouched and braced. She was about sixteen inches high and weighed twenty-two pounds. Her coat was red and silky, and there was a blaze of white down her chest and a circle of white around her throat. Her face was wrinkled and sad, like a wise old man's.

Jesse shook his head. "Looks like a mixture of bloodhound and terrier from here," he whispered. "It beats me—"

"It's a dog, all right," Skeeter said.

"Can't no dog laugh."

"That dog can." The boy began walking toward the animal, his right hand outstretched. "Heah. Heah. I ain't gonna hurt you."

The dog, for she was a dog, cocked her head from one side to the other and watched Skeeter. She was trembling, but she didn't run. And when Skeeter knelt by her, she stopped trembling, for the ways of a boy with a dog are mysterious. He stroked her, and the trim little creature looked up at him and blinked her big hazel eyes. Then she turned over and Skeeter scratched her. She closed her eyes, stretched and chuckled, a happy mixture of chortle and yodel. Jesse ambled up, and the dog leaped to her feet and sprang between the boy and the man.

Skeeter calmed her. "That's just Uncle Jess."

Jesse, still bewildered, shook his head again. "I still say that ain't no dog. She don't smell and she don't bark. Ain't natural. And look at her! Licking herself like a cat."

"Well, I'll be a catty wampus," Skeeter said. "Never saw a dog do that before." However, he was quick to defend any mannerism of his friend and said, "She likes to keep herself clean. She's a lady and I'm gonna name her that, and she's mine 'cause I found her."

"Lady, huh?"

"No, sir. My Lady. If I name her just plain Lady, how folks gonna know she's mine?" He began stroking his dog again. "Gee m'netty, Uncle Jess, I ain't never had nothing like this before."

"It still don't make sense to me," Jesse said. But he didn't care, for he was happy because the child was happy.

Like most mysteries, there was no mystery at all about My Lady. She was a lady all right, an aristocrat Basenji, one of those strange barkless dogs of Africa. Her ancestors were pets of the Pharoahs, and her line was well established when the now-proud races of men were wandering about Europe, begging handouts from Nature. A bundle of nerves and muscles, she would fight anything and could scent game up to eighty yards. She had the gait of an antelope and was odorless, washing herself before and after meals. However the only noises she could make were a piercing cry that sounded almost human and that little chortle. She could chuckle only when happy, and she had been happy in the woods. Now she was happy again.

As most men judge values, she was worth more than all the possessions of Jesse and his nephew. Several of the dogs had been shipped to New Orleans, thence by motor to a northern kennel. While crossing Mississippi, My Lady had escaped from the station wagon. Her keeper had advertised in several papers, but Jesse and Skeeter never saw papers.

Skeeter said, "Come on, M'Lady. Let's go home."

The dog didn't hesitate, but walked proudly at the boy's side to a cabin on the bank of the bayou. Skeeter crumbled corn bread, wet it with pot liquor, and put it before her. She sniffed the food disdainfully at first, then ate it only when she saw the boy fix a bowl for his uncle. She licked herself clean and explored the cabin, sniffing the brush brooms, the piles of wild pecans and hickory nuts, and then the cots. Satisfied at last, she jumped on Skeeter's bed, tucked her nose under her paws, and went to sleep.

"Acts like she owned the place," Jesse said.

"Where you reckon she came from?" The boy slipped his overall straps from his shoulders, flexed his stringy muscles, and yawned.

"Lord knows. Circus maybe." He looked at M'Lady quickly. "Say, maybe she's a freak and run off from some show. Bet they'd give us two dollars for her."

Skeeter's face got long. "You don't aim to get rid of her?"

The old man put his shotgun over the mantel and lit his

pipe. "Skeets, if you want that thing, I wouldn't get shed of her for a piece of bottomland a mile long. Already plowed and planted."

"I reckoned you wouldn't, 'cause you like me so much. And I know how you like dogs, 'cause I saw you cry when yours got killed. But you can have part of mine."

Jesse sat down and leaned back, blowing smoke into the air to drive away mosquitoes. The boy got a brick and hammer and began cracking nuts, pounding the meat to pulp so his uncle could chew it. Skeeter's yellow hair hadn't been cut for months and was tangled. He had freckles too. And his real name was Jonathan. His mother was Jesse's only sister and died when the child was born. No one thereabouts ever knew what happened to his father. Jesse, a leathery, toothless old man with faded blue eyes, took him to bring up and called him Skeeter because he was so little.

In the village, where Jesse seldom visited, folks wondered if he were fit to rear a little boy. They considered him shiftless and no-account. Jesse had lived all of his sixty years in the swamp, and his way of life was a torment to folks who believed life must be lived by rules. He earned a few dollars selling jumbo frogs and pelts, but mostly he just paddled around the swamp, watching things and teaching Skeeter about life.

The villagers might have tried to send Skeeter to an orphanage, but for Joe (Cash) Watson, the storekeeper. Cash was a hard man, but fair. He often hunted with Jesse, and the old man had trained Cash's dogs. When there was talk of sending Skeeter away, Cash said, "You ain't gonna do it. You just don't take young'uns away from their folks." And that's all there was to it.

Jesse never coveted the "frills and furbelows of damn-fool folks" and yearned for only two things—a twenty-gauge shotgun for Skeeter and a set of Roebuckers for himself, as he called store-bought teeth. Cash had promised him the gun and the best false teeth in the catalogue for forty-six dollars. Jesse had saved nine dollars and thirty-seven cents.

"Someday I'm gonna get them Roebuckers," he often told Skeeter. "Then I'm gonna eat me enough roastin' ears to kill a goat. Maybe I can get a set with a couple of gold teeth in 'em. I seen a man once with six gold teeth."

Once Skeeter asked him, "Why don't you get a job with the W.P. and A. and make enough money to buy them Roebuckers?"

"I don't want them that bad," Jesse said.

So he was happy for Skeeter to have M'Lady, thinking the dog would sort of make up for the shotgun.

The boy cracked as many nuts as his uncle wanted, then put the hammer away. He was undressing when he glanced over at his dog. "Gosh, Uncle Jess, I'm scared somebody'll come get her."

"I ain't heard of nobody losing no things around here. If'n they had, they'd been to me 'fore now, being's I know all about dogs and the swamp."

"That's so," Skeeter said, "but you don't reckon she belonged to another fellow like me, do you? I know how I'd feel if I had a dog like her and she got lost."

Jesse said, "She didn't belong to another fellow like you. If'n she had, she wouldn't be so happy here."

Skeeter fed M'Lady biscuits and molasses for breakfast, and although the Basenji ate them, she still was hungry when she went into the swamp with the boy. He was hoping he could find a bee tree or signs of wild hogs. They were at the edge of a clearing when M'Lady's chokebore nose suddenly tilted and she froze to a flash point, pausing only long enough to get set. Then she darted to the bayou, at least sixty yards away, dived into a clump of reeds, and snatched a water rat. She was eating when Skeeter ran up.

"Don't do that," he scolded. "Ain't you got no more sense than run into water after things? A snake or a gator might snatch you."

The Basenji dropped the rat and ducked her head. She knew the boy was displeased, and when she looked up at him, her eyes were filled and a woebegone expression was on her face.

Skeeter tried to explain. "I didn't mean to hurt your feelings. Don't cry." He stepped back quickly and stared at her, at the tears in her eyes. "She *is* crying! Be John Brown!" Skeeter called her and ran toward the cabin, where Jesse was cutting splinters.

"Uncle Jess! Guess what else my dog can do!"

"Whistle?" The old man laughed.

"She can cry! I declare to goodness! Not out loud, but she can cry just the same."

Jesse knew that most dogs will get watery-eyed on occasion, but not wanting to ridicule M'Lady's accomplishments asked, "What made her cry?"

"Well, sir, we were walking along and all of a sudden she got a scent and flash pointed and then—" Skeeter remembered something.

"Then what?"

Skeeter sat on the steps. "Uncle Jess," he said slowly, "we must have been fifty or sixty yards from that rat when she smelled it."

"What rat? What's eating you?"

The child told him the story, and Jesse couldn't believe it. For a dog to pick up the scent of a water rat at sixty yards simply wasn't credible. Jesse reckoned Skeeter's love for M'Lady had led him to exaggerate.

Skeeter knew Jesse didn't believe the story, so he said, "Come on. I'll show you." He whistled for M'Lady.

The dog came up. "Hey," Jesse said. "That thing knows what a whistle means. Shows she's been around folks." He caught the dog's eye and commanded, "Heel!"

But M'Lady cocked her head quizzically. Then she turned to the boy and chuckled softly. She'd never heard the order before. That was obvious. Her nose came up into the breeze and she wheeled. Her curved tail suddenly was still, and her head was poised.

"Flash pointing," Jesse said. "Well, I'll be a monkey's uncle!"

M'Lady held the strange point only for a second, though, then dashed toward a corn patch about eighty yards from the cabin. Halfway to the patch, she broke her gait and began creeping. A whir of feathered lightning sounded in the corn, and a covey of quail exploded almost under her nose. She sprang and snatched a bird.

"Partridges!" Jesse's jaw dropped.

The child was as motionless as stone, his face white and his eyes wide in amazement. Finally he found his voice. "She was right here when she smelled them birds. A good eighty yards."

"I know she ain't no dog now," Jesse said. "Can't no dog do that."

"She's fast as greased lightning and ain't scared of nothin."

Skeeter still was under the spell of the adventure. "She's a hunting dog from way back."

"She aint' no dog a-tall, I'm telling you. It ain't human." Jesse walked toward M'Lady and told her to fetch the bird, but the dog didn't understand. Instead, she pawed it. "Well," Jesse said. "One thing's certain. She ain't no bird hunter."

"She can do anything," Skeeter said. "Even hunt birds. Maybe I can make a bird dog out'n her. Wouldn't that be som'n?"

"You're batty. Maybe a coon dog, but not a bird dog. I know about dogs."

"Me too," said Skeeter. And he did. He'd seen Jesse train many dogs, even pointers, and had helped him train Big Boy, Cash Watson's prize gun dog.

Jesse eyed Skeeter and read his mind. "It can't be done, Skeets."

"Maybe not, but I aim to try. Any dog can run coons and rabbits, but it takes a puredee humdinger to hunt birds. Ain't no sin in trying, is it?"

"Naw," Jesse said slowly, "but she'll flush birds."

"I'll learn her not to."

"She won't hold no point. Any dog'll flash point. And she'll hunt rats."

"I'm gonna learn her just to hunt birds. And I'm starting right now," Skeeter said. He started walking away, then turned. "I seen a man once train a razorback hawg to point birds. You know as good as me that if a dog's got puredee hoss sense and a fellow's got bat brains, he can train the dog to hunt birds."

"Wanta bet?" Jesse issued the challenge in an effort to

keep Skeeter's enthusiasm and determination at the high-water mark.

"Yes, sir. If I don't train my dog, then I'll cut all the splinters for a year. If I do, you cut 'em.'"

"It's a go," Jesse said.

Skeeter ran to the bayou and recovered the rat M'Lady had killed. He tied it around his dog's neck. The Basenji was indignant and tried to claw off the hateful burden. Failing, she ran into the house and under a bed, but Skeeter made her come out. M'Lady filled up then, and her face assumed that don't-nobody-love-me look. The boy steeled himself, tapped M'Lady's nose with the rat, and left it around her neck.

"You done whittled out a job for yourself," Jesse said. "If'n you get her trained, you'll lose her in the brush. She's too fast and too little to keep up with."

"I'll bell her," Skeeter said. "I'm gonna learn her ever'-thing. I got us a gun dog, Uncle Jess."

The old man sat on the porch, propped against the wall. "Bud, I don't know what that thing is. But you're a thoroughbred. John dog my hide!"

If Skeeter had loved M'Lady one bit less, his patience would have exploded during the ordeal of training the Basenji. It takes judgment and infinite patience to train a bird dog properly, but to train a Basenji, which will hunt anything, to concentrate only on quail took something more than discipline and patience. It never could have been done except for that strange affinity between a boy and a dog and the blind faith of a child.

M'Lady's devotion to Skeeter was so complete that she

was anxious to do anything to earn a pat. It wasn't difficult to teach her to heel and follow at Skeeter's feet regardless of the urge to dash away and chase rabbits. The boy used a clothesline as a guide rope and made M'Lady follow him. The first time the dog tried to chase an animal, Skeeter pinched the rope around her neck just a bit and commanded, "Heel!" When she obeyed, Skeeter released the noose. It took M'Lady only a few hours to associate disobedience with disfavor.

The dog learned that when she chased and killed a rat or rabbit, the thing would be tied around her neck. The only things she could hunt without being disciplined were quail. Of course, she often mistook the scent of game chickens for quail and hunted them, but Skeeter punished her by scolding. He never switched his dog, but to M'Lady a harsh word from the boy hurt more than a hickory limb.

Jesse watched the dog's progress and pretended not to be impressed. He never volunteered suggestions. M'Lady learned quickly, but the task of teaching her to point birds seemed hopeless. Skeeter knew she'd never point as pointers do, so he worked out his own system. He taught her to stand motionless when he shouted, "Hup!" One day she got a scent of birds, paused or pointed for a moment as most animals will, and was ready to spring away when Skeeter said, "Hup!"

M'Lady was confused. Every instinct urged her to chase the birds, but her master had said stand still. She broke, however, and Skeeter scolded her. She pouted at first, then filled up, but the boy ignored her until she obeyed the next command. Then he patted her and she chuckled.

The lessons continued for weeks, and slowly and surely

M'Lady learned her chores. She learned that the second she smelled birds she must stop and stand still until Skeeter flushed them. That she must not quiver when he shot.

Teaching her to fetch was easy, but teaching her to retrieve dead birds without damaging them was another matter. M'Lady had a hard mouth, that is, she sank her teeth into the birds. Skeeter used one of the oldest hunting tricks of the backwoods to break her.

He got a stick and wrapped it with wire and taught his dog to fetch it. Only once did M'Lady bite hard on the stick, and then the wire hurt her sensitive mouth. Soon she developed a habit of carrying the stick on her tongue and supporting it lightly with her teeth. Skeeter tied quail feathers on the stick, and soon M'Lady's education was complete.

Skeeter led Jesse into a field one day and turned his dog loose. She flashed to a point almost immediately. It was a funny point and Jesse almost laughed. The dog's curved tail poked up over her back, she spraddled her front legs and sort of squatted, her nose pointing the birds more than forty yards away. She remained rigid until the boy flushed and shot; then she leaped away, seeking and fetching dead birds.

Jesse was mighty proud. "Well, Skeets, looks like you got yourself a bird hunter."

"Yes, sir," Skeeter said. "And you got yourself a job." He pointed toward the kindling pile.

The swamp was dressing for winter when Cash Watson drove down that day to give his Big Boy a workout in the wild brush.

He fetched Jesse a couple of cans of smoking tobacco

and Skeeter a bag of peppermint jawbreakers. He locked
his fine pointer in the corncrib for the night and was warming himself in the cabin when he noticed M'Lady for the
first time. She was sleeping in front of the fire.

"What's that?" he asked.

"My dog," said Skeeter. "Ain't she a beaut?"

"She sure is." Cash grinned at Jesse. Skeeter went out to
the well, and Cash asked his old friend, "What the devil
kind of mutt is that?"

"Search me," Jesse said. "Skeets found her in the swamp.
I reckon she's got a trace of bloodhound in her and some
terrier and a heap of just plain dog."

M'Lady cocked one ear, got up, and stretched; then,
apparently not liking the company, she turned her tail
toward Cash and strutted out, looking for Skeeter.

The men laughed. "Som'n wrong with her throat," Jesse
said. "She can't bark. When she tries, she makes a funny
sound, sort of a cackling, chuckling yodel. Sounds like she's
laughing."

"Well," Cash said, "trust a young'un to love the orner'st
dog he can find."

"Wait a minute," Jesse said. "She ain't no-count. She's a
bird-hunting fool."

Just then Skeeter entered, and Cash jestingly said, "Hear
you got yourself a bird dog, son."

The boy clasped his hands behind him and rocked on
the balls of his feet as he had seen the men do. "Well now,
I'll tell you, Mr. Cash. M'Lady does ever'thing except tote
the gun."

"She must be fair to middling. Why not take her out
with Big Boy tomorrow? Do my dog good to hunt in a
brace."

"Me and my dog don't want to show Big Boy up. He's a pretty good ol' dog."

"Whoa!" Cash was every inch a bird-dog man, and nobody could challenge him without a showdown. Besides, Skeeter was shooting up and should be learning a few things about life. "Any old boiler can pop off steam." Cash winked at Jesse.

"Well now, sir, if you're itching for a run, I'll just double-dog dare you to run your dog against mine. And anybody who'll take a dare will pull up young cotton and push a widow woman's ducks in the water."

Cash admired the boy's confidence. "All right, son. It's a deal. What are the stakes?"

Skeeter started to mention the twenty-gauge gun he wanted, but changed his mind quickly. He reached down and patted M'Lady, then looked up. "If my dog beats yours, then you get them Roebuckers for Uncle Jess."

Jesse's chest suddenly was tight. Cash glanced from the boy to the man, and he too was proud of Skeeter. "I wasn't aiming to go that high. But all right. What do I get if I win?"

"I'll cut you ten cords of stovewood."

"And a stack of splinters?"

"Yes, sir."

Cash offered his hand and Skeeter took it. "It's a race," Cash said. "Jesse will be the judge."

The wind was rustling the sage and there was a nip in the early-morning air when they took the dogs to a clearing and set them down. Skeeter snapped a belt around M'Lady's neck, and at word from Jesse the dogs were released.

Big Boy bounded away and began circling, ranging into the brush. M'Lady tilted her nose into the wind and ripped away toward the sage, her bell tinkling. Cash said, "She sure covers ground." Skeeter made no effort to keep up with her, but waited until he couldn't hear the bell, then ran for a clearing where he had last heard it. And there was M'Lady on a point.

Cash almost laughed out loud. "That ain't no point, son. That's a squat."

"She's got birds."

"Where?"

Jesse leaned against a tree and watched the fun.

Skeeter pointed toward a clump of sage. "She's pointing birds in that sage."

Cash couldn't restrain his mirth. "Boy, now that's what I call some pointing. Why, Skeeter, it's sixty or seventy yards to that sage."

Just then Big Boy flashed by M'Lady, his head high. He raced to the edge of the sage, caught the wind, then whipped around, freezing to a point. Cash called Jesse's attention to the point.

"That's M'Lady's point," Skeeter said. "She's got the same birds Big Boy has."

Jesse sauntered up. "The boy's right, Cash. I aimed to keep my mouth out'n this race, but M'Lady is pointing them birds. She can catch scents up to eighty yards."

Cash said, "Aw, go on, you're crazy." He walked over and flushed the birds.

Skeeter picked one off and ordered M'Lady to fetch. When she returned with the bird, the boy patted her and she began chuckling.

Cash really studied her then for the first time. "Hey!" he said suddenly. "A Basenji! That's a Basenji!"

"A what?" Jesse asked.

"I should have known." Cash was very excited. "That's the dog that was lost by them rich Yankees. I saw about it in the paper." He happened to look at Skeeter then and wished he had cut out his tongue.

The boy's lips were compressed, and his face was drawn and white. Jesse had closed his eyes and was rubbing his forehead.

Cash, trying to dismiss the subject, said, "Just 'cause it was in the paper don't make it so. I don't believe that's the same dog, come to think of it."

"Do you aim to tell 'em where the dog is?" Skeeter asked.

Cash looked at Jesse, then at the ground. "It ain't none of my business."

"How about you, Uncle Jess?"

"I ain't telling nobody nothin'."

"I know she's the same dog," Skeeter said, "on account of I just know it. But she's mine now." His voice rose and trembled. "And ain't nobody gonna take her away from me." He ran into the swamp. M'Lady was at his heels.

Cash said, "Durn my lip. I'm sorry, Jesse. If I'd kept my big mouth shut, he'd never known the difference."

"It can't be helped now," Jesse said.

"Course she beat Big Boy. Them's the best hunting dogs in the world. And she's worth a mint of money."

They didn't feel up to hunting and returned to the cabin and sat on the porch. Neither had much to say, but kept glancing toward the swamp where Skeeter and M'Lady were walking along the bayou.

"Don't you worry," Skeeter said tenderly. "Ain't nobody gonna bother you."

He sat on a stump and M'Lady put her head on his

knee. She wasn't worrying. Nothing could have been more contented than she was.

"I don't care if the sheriff comes down." Skeeter pulled her on his lap and held her. "I don't give a whoop if the governor comes down. Even the president of the United States! The whole shebang can come, but ain't nobody gonna mess with you."

His words gave him courage and he felt better, but for only a minute. Then the tug-of-war between him and his conscience started.

"Once I found a Barlow knife and kept it, and it was all right," he mumbled.

But this is different.

"Finders, keepers; losers, weepers."

No, Skeeter.

"Well, I don't care. She's mine."

Remember what your Uncle Jess said.

"He said a heap of things."

Yes, but you remember one thing more than the rest. He said, "Certain things are right and certain things are wrong. And nothing ain't gonna ever change that. When you learn that, then you're fit'n to be a man." Remember, Skeeter?

A feeling of despair and loneliness almost overwhelmed him. He fought off the tears as long as he could, but finally he gave in, and his sobs caused M'Lady to peer into his face and wonder why he was acting that way when she was so happy. He put his arms around her neck and pulled her to him. "My li'l old puppy dog. Poor li'l old puppy dog. But I got to do it."

He sniffed back his tears and got up and walked to the

cabin. M'Lady curled up by the fire and the boy sat down, watching the logs splutter for several minutes. Then he said almost in a whisper, "Uncle Jess, if you keep som'n that ain't yours, it's the same as stealing, ain't it?"

Cash leaned against the mantel and stared into the fire. Jesse puffed his pipe slowly. "Son, that's som'n you got to settle with yourself."

Skeeter stood and turned his back to the flames, warming his hands. "Mr. Cash," he said slowly, "when you get back to your store, please let them folks know their dog is here."

"If that's how it is—"

"That's how it is," Skeeter said.

The firelight dancing on Jesse's face revealed the old man's dejection, and Skeeter, seeing it, said quickly, "It's best for M'Lady. She's too good for the swamp. They'll give her a good home."

Jesse flinched, and Cash, catching the hurt look in his friend's eyes, said, "Your dog outhunted mine, Skeets. You win them Roebuckers for your uncle."

"I don't want 'em," Jesse said, rather childishly. "I don't care if'n I never eat no roastin' ears." He got up quickly and hurried outside. Cash reckoned he'd better be going and left Skeeter by the fire, rubbing his dog.

Jesse came back in directly and pulled up a chair. Skeeter started to speak, but Jesse spoke first. "I been doing a heap of thinking lately. You're sprouting up. The swamp ain't no place for you."

Skeeter forgot about his dog and faced his uncle, bewildered.

"I reckon you're too good for the swamp too," Jesse said. "I'm aiming to send you into town for a spell. I can

make enough to keep you in fit'n clothes and all." He dared
not look at the boy.

"Uncle Jess!" Skeeter said reproachfully. "You don't mean
that. You're just saying that on account of what I said about
M'Lady. I said it just to keep you from feeling so bad about
our dog going away. Gee m'netty, Uncle Jess. I ain't ever
gonna leave you." He buried his face in his uncle's shoulder.
M'Lady put her head on Jesse's knee, and he patted the
boy and rubbed the dog.

"Reckon I'll take them Roebuckers," he said at last. "I
been wanting some for a long, long time."

Several days later Cash drove down and told them the
man from the kennels was at his store. Skeeter didn't say a
word, but called M'Lady and they got in Cash's car. All the
way to town the boy was silent. He held his dog's head in
his lap.

The keeper took just one look at M'Lady and said, "That's
she, all right. Miss Congo III." He turned to speak to
Skeeter, but the boy was walking away. He got a glance
at Skeeter's face, however. "Hell," he muttered, "I wish
you fellows hadn't told me. I hate to take his dog away."

"He wanted you to know," Cash said.

"Mister"—Jesse closed his left eye and struck his swap-
ping pose—"I'd like to swap you out'n that hound. Now,
course, she ain't much 'count. . . ."

The keeper smiled in spite of himself. "If she was mine,
I'd give her to the child. But she's not for sale. The owner
wants to breed her and establish her line in this country.
And if she was for sale, she'd cost more money than any
of us will ever see."

He called Skeeter and offered his hand. Skeeter shook it. "You're a good kid. There's a reward for this dog."

"I don't want no reward." The boy's words tumbled out. "I don't want nothing except to be left alone. You've got your dog, mister. Take her and go on. Please." He walked away again, fearing he would cry.

Cash said, "I'll take the reward and keep it for him. Someday he'll want it."

Jesse went out to the store porch to be with Skeeter. The keeper handed Cash the money. "It's tough, but the kid'll get over it. The dog never will."

"Is that a fact?"

"Yep. I know the breed. They never forget. That dog'll never laugh again. They never laugh unless they're happy."

He walked to the post where Skeeter had tied M'Lady. He untied the leash and started toward his station wagon. M'Lady braced her front feet and looked around for the boy. Seeing him on the porch, she jerked away from the keeper and ran to her master.

She rubbed against his legs. Skeeter tried to ignore her. The keeper reached for the leash again, and M'Lady crouched, baring her fangs. The keeper shrugged, a helpless gesture. "Wild elephants couldn't pull that dog away from that boy," he said.

"That's all right, mister." Skeeter unsnapped the leash and tossed it to the keeper. Then he walked to the station wagon, opened the door of a cage, and called, "Heah, M'Lady!" She bounded to him. "Up!" he commanded. She didn't hesitate, but leaped into the cage. The keeper locked the door.

M'Lady, having obeyed a command, poked her nose between the bars, expecting a pat. The boy rubbed her head. She tried to move closer to him, but the bars held her. She looked quizzically at the bars, then tried to nudge them aside. Then she clawed them. A look of fear suddenly came to her eyes, and she fastened them on Skeeter, wistfully at first, then pleadingly. She couldn't make a sound, for her unhappiness had sealed her throat. Slowly her eyes filled up.

"Don't cry no more, M'Lady. Ever'thing's gonna be all right." He reached out to pat her, but the station wagon moved off, leaving him standing there in the dust.

Back on the porch, Jesse lit his pipe and said to his friend, "Cash, the boy has lost his dog, and I've lost a boy."

"Aw, Jesse, Skeeter wouldn't leave you."

"That ain't what I mean. He's growed up, Cash. He don't look no older, but he is. He growed up that day in the swamp."

Skeeter walked into the store, and Cash followed him. "I've got that reward for you, Jonathan."

It was the first time anyone ever had called him that, and it sounded like man talk.

"And that twenty gauge is waiting for you," Cash said. "I'm gonna give it to you."

"Thank you, Mr. Cash." The boy bit his lower lip. "But I don't aim to do no more hunting. I don't never want no more dogs."

"Know how you feel. But if you change your mind, the gun's here for you."

Skeeter looked back toward the porch where Jesse was waiting and said, "Tell you what, though. When you get them Roebuckers, get some with a couple of gold teeth in 'em. Take it out of the reward money."

"Sure, Jonathan."

Jesse joined them, and Skeeter said, "We better be getting back toward the house."

"I'll drive you down," Cash said. "But first I aim to treat you to some lemon pop and sardines."

"That's mighty nice of you," Jesse said, "but we better be gettin' on."

"What's the hurry?" Cash opened the pop.

"It's my time to cut splinters," Jesse said. "That's what I get for betting with a good man."

The Dog That Traveled
Incognito   *Ludwig Bemelmans*

"Look what a lovely day we have for sailing," I said, pointing my pen toward the sunlit greenery outside the open
window. Birds sang in trees, and the sun shone on a pack
of brightly colored baggage tags that I was filling out.
Under *SS America*, I had carefully lettered my name, and
I answered the gay question, Destination?, with Cherbourg.

I was about to fill out a new tag when I noticed Barbara's
silence. I looked up at her. She was standing at the window
looking at me. I remembered that on the day before she had
said something about a dog, but I had been called away
before I could talk about it at length.

For the most part, Barbara is a sweet and normal child. When she wants something, she changes. I looked at her now and clearly saw the symptoms of wanting something, symptoms long known to me and always the same. I recognized the first stage of a painful condition that overcomes her from time to time. I saw that this time it would be very grave and complicated. I could tell it by her eyes, her mouth, the position she stood in, the peculiar angles of her arms and legs. She was twisted in an unhappy pose of indecision. Not that she didn't know precisely what she wanted. Barbara was merely undecided about how to broach the subject. There was a long and cold silence.

At this point the child is always under great stress. A trembling of the lower lip precedes the filling of the beautiful eyes with tears. I am allowed to see these hopeless eyes for a moment, and then, as a spotlight moves from one place to another, she averts her gaze and slowly turns, folds her arms, and looks into the distance or, if there is no distance, at the wall. The crisis is approaching. She swallows, but her throat is constricted. Finally, with the urgency of a stammerer and with her small hands clenched, she manages to say a few dry words. Her voice is like a cold trumpet; the last word is a choking sound.

This morning—the morning we were sailing—the attack was particularly severe. After the silence, the tears, and the gaze into the distance, Barbara blurted out, "You promised I could have a dog."

I steeled myself and answered, "Yes, when we get back from Europe you can have a dog."

An answer like that is worse than an outright no. The mood of "I wish I were dead" descended on Barbara. She stared coldly out the window, and then she turned and limply dragged herself down the corridor to her room, where she goes at times of crisis. She closed the door, not by slamming it, but with a terrible, slow finality. From the corridor I could see how she let go of the doorknob inside. In an unspeakably dolorous fashion, the knob slowly turned, and there was a barely audible click of the mechanism. It was a cutting off of human relations, a falling off of appetite, and nothing of joy or disaster in all the world mattered to her.

Ordinarily this comatose state lasts for weeks. In this case, however, Barbara was confronted with a deadline, for the ship was sailing at five that afternoon, and it was now eleven in the morning. I usually break down after three or four weeks of resistance. The time limit for this operation was five hours.

For a while she continued to follow the manual of standard practice, which I know like the alphabet. From the door at the end of the corridor came the sound of heartbreaking sobs. Normally these sobs last for a good while; then, the crisis ebbing, there follows an hour or two of real or simulated sleep, in which she gathers strength for new efforts. This time, however, the sobs were discontinued ahead of schedule. There was a period of total silence, during which I knew she was plotting at the speed of a calculating machine. This took about ten minutes. Then the door opened again, and fatefully and slowly as the condemned walk to their place of execution, the poor child, handkerchief in hand, dragged along the corridor and passed me in phantomlike silence and, in a wide half circle, passed into the kitchen. I never knew until that morning that pouring milk into a glass could be a bitter and hopeless thing to watch.

I am as hardened to the heartbreak routine as a coroner is to postmortems. I can be blind to tears and deaf to the most urgent pleading. I said, "Please be reasonable. I promise you that the moment we get back you can have a dog."

I was not prepared for what followed: the new slant, the surprise attack. She leaned against the kitchen door-frame and drank the last of the milk. Her mouth was ringed with white. Then she said in measured and accusing tones, "You read in the papers this morning what they did in Albany?"

"I beg your pardon?"

"They passed a law that all institutions like the SPCA are forced to turn dogs over to hospitals for vivisection— and you know what will happen. They'll get him, and then they'll cut him open and sew him up again, over and over, until he's dead."

"What has that got to do with me?"

"It has to do with the dog you promised me."

"What dog?"

"The dog that Frances wants to give me."

Frances is a redheaded girl who goes to school with Barbara.

"I didn't know Frances had a dog."

Barbara raised her eyebrows. "You never listen." And, with weary gestures as if she were talking to an idiot, she said, "Poppy, I told you all about it a dozen times. Dr. Lincoln—that's Frances's father—is going to Saudi Arabia to work for an oil company, and he had to sign a paper agreeing not to take a dog, because it seems the Arabs don't like dogs. So the dog has to be got rid of. So Dr. Lincoln said, 'If you don't get rid of it, I will.' Now you know how doctors are. They have no feelings whatever for animals. He'll give it to some hospital for experiments."

I resumed filling out baggage tags. When I hear the word *dog* I think of a reasonably large animal of no particular breed, uncertain in outline like a Thurber dog, and with a rough, dark coat. This image hovered in my mind when I asked, "What kind of a dog is it?"

"Its name is Little Bit."

"What?"

"Little Bit, that's its name. It's the dearest, sweetest, snow-white, itsy-bitsy toy poodle you have ever seen. Can I have it? Please?"

I almost let out a shrill bark.

"Wait till you see him and all the things he's got: a special little wicker bed with a mattress, and he has a dish with his picture on it, and around it is written *Always Faithful* in French. You see, Poppy, they got him in Paris last year, and he's the uniquest, sharpest little dog you have ever seen, and of course he is housebroken, and Frances says she's not going to give him to anybody but me."

I was playing for time. I would have settled for a corgi, a Yorkshire, a Weimaraner, even a German boxer or a Mexican hairless, but Little Bit was too much. I knew that Dr. Lincoln lived some thirty miles out of New York, and that it would be impossible for him to get the dog to New York before the ship sailed.

"Where is the dog now?" I asked.

"He'll be here any minute, Poppy. Frances is on the way with him now. And, oh, wait till you see. He has the cutest little boots for rainy weather, and a cashmere sweater, sea green, and several sets of leashes and collars. You won't have to buy anything for him."

"All right," I said, "you can have him. We'll put him in a good kennel until we get back."

The symptoms, well known and always the same, returned again. The low lip trembled. "Kennel," she said, and there is no actress on the stage who could have weighted this word with more reproach and misery.

"Yes, kennel," I said, and I filled out the baggage tag for my portable typewriter.

"Poppy—" she began.

But I got up and said, "Now look, Barbara, the ship leaves in a few hours, and to take a dog aboard you have to get a certificate from a veterinary, and reserve a place for him, and buy a ticket."

To my astonishment, Barbara smiled indulgently and said, "Well, if that's all that is bothering you— First of all, the French, unlike the English, have no quarantine for dogs, and Little Bit already has a certificate. Second, you can make all the arrangements for a dog's passage on board ship after it sails. Third, there is plenty of room in the ship's kennels. I know all this because Frances and I went down to the U.S. Lines office and got this information day before yesterday."

As such times I feel for the boy who will someday marry Barbara. With all hope failing, I said, "But we'll have to get a traveling bag or something to put the dog in."

"He has a lovely little traveling bag with his name lettered on it, *Little Bit*."

The name stung like a whip. "All right then." I wrote an extra baggage tag for the dog's bag.

Barbara wore the smug smile of success. "Wait till you see him," she said, and she ran downstairs. She returned with Frances, who, I am sure, had been sitting there waiting all the time.

Little Bit had shoe-button eyes and a patent-leather nose and a strawberry-colored collar. He was fluffy from the top of his head to his shoulders and then shorn like a miniature Persian lamb. At the end of a stub of a tail was a puff of fluff, and there were other puffs on his four legs. He wore a red ribbon and a bell on his collar. I thought that sawdust would come out of him if he were cut open.

A real dog moves about a room and sniffs his way into corners; he inspects furniture and people and makes notes of things. Little Bit stood with cock-sparrow stiffness on four legs, as static as his stare. He was picked up and brought over to me, and I think he knew exactly what I thought of him, for he lifted his tiny lip on the left side of his face up over his mouselike teeth and sneered. He was put down, and he danced on stilts, with the motion of a mechanical toy, back to Frances.

I was shown the traveling bag, which was like one of the pocketbooks that Wacs carry.

"We don't need that tag," Barbara said. "I'll carry him in this. Look." She opened the pocketbook, which had a circular opening with a wire screen on both ends for breathing purposes, Little Bit jumped into it, and she closed it. "You see, he won't be any bother whatever."

She opened the bag again, and, with a standing jump, Little Bit hurdled its handles. He stalked toward me and, tilting his head a little, looked up at me, and then he again lifted his lip over his small fangs.

"Oh, look, Barbara," said Frances. "Little Bit likes your father. He's smiling at him." I had an impulse to sneer back, but instead I took the baggage tags and began to attach them to the luggage.

I left the room then, for now Frances showed signs of crisis; her eyes were filling, and the heartbreak was too much for me.

Little Bit was less emotional. He ate a hearty meal from his *Toujours Fidèle* dish. Then he inspected the house, tinkling about with the small bell that hung from his patent-leather collar.

It was time to leave for the boat. The baggage was taken to a taxi, and Little Bit hopped into his bag. On the way to the boat I thought about the things I had forgotten to take care of, and also about Little Bit. It is said that there are three kinds of books that are always a success; they are a book about a doctor, a book about Lincoln, and a book about a dog. Well, now I had Dr. Lincoln's dog, but the situation didn't seem to hold the elements of anything except chagrin. I wondered if Lincoln ever had had a dog, or a doctor, or if Lincoln's doctor had a dog. I wondered if that side of Lincoln, perhaps the last remaining side, had been investigated yet or was still open.

We arrived with Dr. Lincoln's dog at the customs barrier, our passports were checked, and the baggage was brought aboard. In the cabin we found some friends. Little Frances, with Barbara and Little Bit, looking out of his bag, inspected the ship. The gong sounded and the deck steward sang, "All ashore that's going ashore." The passengers lined up to wave their farewells. The last of those that were going ashore hurried down the gangplank (good-by, good-by!), and then the engine bells sounded below. The tugs moaned and hissed, and the ship backed out into the river. There are few sights in the world as beautiful as a trip down the

Hudson and out to sea, especially at dusk. I was on deck until we were in Ambrose Channel, and then I went down into the cabin.

Little Bit was lying on the writing desk on a blotter and watching Barbara's hand. She was writing a letter to Frances, describing the beauty of travel and Little Bit's reactions. "Isn't he the best traveling dog we've ever had, Poppy?"

The cabins aboard the *America* are the only ones I have ever been in that don't seem to be aboard ship. They are large, like rooms in a country home, and a little chintzy in decoration. The portholes are curtained, and in back of the curtains, one suspects, screened doors lead out to a porch and a Connecticut lawn rather than the ocean.

I put my things in place and changed into a comfortable jacket, and then I said, "I guess I'd better go up and get this dog business settled."

"It's all attended to, Poppy. I took care of it," said Barbara, and she continued writing.

"Well, then, you'd better take him upstairs to the kennels now. It's almost dinner time."

"He doesn't have to go to the kennels."

"Now, look, Barbara—"

"See for yourself, Poppy. Ring for the steward, or let me ring for him."

"Yes, sir," said the steward, smiling.

"Is it all right for the dog to stay in the cabin?" I asked. The steward had one of the most honest and kind faces I have ever seen. He didn't fit on a ship either. He was more like a person that works around horses or a gardener. He had bright eyes and squint lines, a leathery skin, and a good smile. He closed his eyes and said, "Dog? I don't see no dog in here, sir." He winked like a burlesque comedian and touched one finger to his head in salute. "My name is Jeff," he said. "If you want anything . . ." and he was gone.

"You see?" said Barbara. "And besides, you save fifty dollars, and coming back another fifty makes a hundred."

I am sure that Little Bit understood every word of the conversation. He stood up on the blotter and tilted his head, listening to Barbara. She said to him, "Now you know, Little Bit, you're not supposed to be on this ship at all. You mustn't allow anybody to see you. Now you hide while we go to eat."

There was a knock at the door. Little Bit jumped to the floor, and he was out of sight.

It was the steward. He brought a little raw meat mixed with string beans on a plate and covered with another plate. "Yes, sir," was all he said.

After he left, we took the bell off Little Bit's collar as a precaution.

Barbara was asleep when the first rapport between me and Little Bit took place. I was sitting on a couch, reading, when he came into my cabin. By some magic trick, like an elevator going up a shaft, he ascended and sat down next to me. He kept a hand's width away, tilted his head, and then lifted his lip over the left side of his face. I think I smiled back at him in the same fashion. I looked at him with interest for the first time. He was embarrassed; he looked away and then suddenly changed position, stretching his front legs ahead and sitting down flat on his hind legs. He made several jerky movements but never uttered a sound.

Barbara's sleepy voice came from the other room: "Aren't you glad we've got Little Bit with us?"

"Yes," I said, "I am."

I thought about the miracles of nature: that this tough little lion in sheep's pelt functioned as he did with a brain that could be no larger than an olive; that he had memory, understanding, tact, courage, and, no doubt, loyalty; that he was completely self-sufficient. He smiled once more, and I smiled back; the relationship was established. Life went on as steadily as the ship.

On the afternoon of the third day out, as I lay in my deck chair reading, Barbara came running. "Little Bit is gone," she stammered with trembling lower lip.

We went down to the cabin. The steward was on all fours, looking under the beds and furniture. "Somebody must have left the door open," he said, "or it wasn't closed properly and swung open, and I suppose he got lonesome here all by himself and went looking for you. You should have taken him up to the movies with you, miss."

"He's a smart dog," Barbara said. "Let's go everywhere he might go looking for us."

So we went to the dining room, to the smoking room, the theater, the swimming pool, up the stairs, down the stairs, up on all the decks and around them, and to a secret little deck we had discovered between second and third class, where Little Bit was taken for his exercise mornings and evenings, where he ran about freely while I stood guard. A liner is as big as a city. He was nowhere.

When we got back, the steward said, "I know where he is. You see, anybody finds a dog naturally takes it up to the kennel, and that's the end. He stays for the rest of the trip. Well, remember, I never saw the dog. I don't know about him. The butcher—that's the man in charge of the kennels —he's liable to report me if he finds out I helped hide him. He's mean, especially about money. He figures that each passenger gives him ten bucks for taking care of a dog, and he doesn't want any of us to snatch it.

"There was a Yorkshire stowing away trip before last. He caught him on the gangplank as the dog was leaving the ship. The passenger had put him on a leash. Well, the butcher stopped him from getting off. He held up everything for hours. The man had to pay passage for the dog, and the steward who had helped hide him was fired. Herman Haegeli is his name, and he's as mean as they come. You'll find him on the top deck, near the aft chimney, where it says *Kennel*."

At moments such as this one, I enjoy the full confidence and affection of my child. Her nervous little hand is in mine; she willingly takes direction; she is all devotion, and no trouble is too much. She loves me especially then, because she knows that I am larcenous at heart and willing to go to the greatest lengths to beat a game and especially a meanie. "Now remember," I said, "if you want that dog back we have to be very careful. First, let's go and case the joint."

We climbed up into the scene of white-and-red smokestacks, the sounds of humming wires, and the swish of water. In yellow and crimson fire, the ball of the sun had half sunk into the sea, precisely at the end of the avenue of foam that the ship had plowed in the ocean. We were alone. We walked up and down like people taking exercise before dinner, and the sea changed to violet, and to indigo, and then to that glossy gunmetal hue that it wears on moonless nights. The ship swished along to the even pulse of her machinery.

There was the sign. A yellow light shone from a porthole. I lifted Barbara, and inside, in the immensity of one of the upper cages, was Little Bit, behind bars. There was no lock on his cage; there was no one inside the kennel. The door was fastened by a padlock. We walked back and forth for a while, and then a man came up the stairs carrying a pail. He took the padlock off the door.

"That's our man," I said to Barbara.

Inside the kennel, he brought forth a large dish like the body of a kettledrum. The dogs were barking.

"Now listen carefully, Barbara. I will go in and start a conversation with Mr. Haegeli. I will try to arrange it so that he turns his back on the cage in which Little Bit is, and you carefully open the door of the cage, grab Little Bit, put him under your coat, and then you don't run—you stand still. After a while you say, 'Oh, please, let's get out of here.' I will then say good evening, and we both will leave very slowly. Remember to act calmly, watch the butcher, but don't expect a signal from me. Decide yourself when it is time to act. It may be when he is in the middle of work or while he is talking."

"Oh, please, Poppy. Let's get out of here," Barbara said, rehearsing.

I opened the door to the kennel and smiled like a tourist in appreciation of a new discovery. "Oh, this is where the dogs are kept," I said. "Good evening."

Mr. Haegeli looked up and answered with a grunt. He was mixing dog food.

"My, what nice food you're preparing for them!" I said. "How much do they charge to take a dog across?"

"Fifty dollars," said Mr. Haegeli, who had a Swiss accent. There are all kinds of Swiss, some with French, some with Italian, and some with German accents. They all talk in a singing fashion. Their faces are as varied as their accents. The butcher didn't look like a butcher. A good butcher is fat and rosy. Mr. Haegeli was thin-lipped and thin-nosed. His chin was pointed, and in the light he didn't look as mean as I had expected. He looked rather fanatic and frustrated.

"How often do you feed them?"

"They eat twice a day, and as good as anybody on board," said Mr. Haegeli. "All except Rolfi there. He belongs to an actor, Mr. Gruber. He crosses twice a year, and he brings the dog's food along." He pointed to the cage where a large police dog was housed. "Rolfi, he is fed once a day, out of cans." He seemed to resent Rolfi and his master.

"You exercise them?"

"Yes, of course, all except Rolfi. Mr. Gruber comes up in the morning and takes him around on the top deck, and he sits with him there on a bench. There is such a thing as making too much fuss over a dog."

I said that I agreed with him.

"He tried to keep him in his cabin. He said he'd pay full fare for Rolfi, like a passenger. He'll come up any minute now to say good-night to Rolfi. Some people are crazy about dogs." Mr. Haegeli was putting chopped meat, vegetables, and cereal into the large dish. "There are other people that try and smuggle dogs across, like that one there." He pointed at Little Bit. "But we catch them." He sang it in his Swiss dialect. "Oh, yes, we catch them; they think they're smart, but they don't get away with it, not with me on board they don't. I have ways of finding out. I track them down." The fires of the fanatic burned in his eyes. "I catch them every time." He sounded as if he turned them over to the guillotine after he caught them. "Here comes Mr. Gruber," he said, and opened the door.

Kurt Gruber, the actor, said good evening and introduced himself. He spoke in German to Mr. Haegeli, and Mr. Haegeli turned his back on Little Bit's cage. As he opened Rolfi's cage we were deafened with barking from a dozen cages. The breathless moment had arrived. Barbara was approaching his cage door when the dog lover Gruber saw Little Bit and said, "There's a new one." He spoke to Little Bit, and Little Bit, who had behaved as if he had been carefully rehearsed for his liberation, turned away with tears in his eyes. Mr. Gruber and his dog disappeared.

Herr Haegeli had wiped his hand on his smock and, with it still smeary with dog food, had shaken hands when we introduced ourselves. He was now proceeding to mix the dog food, and the chances for rescuing Little Bit were getting slim.

"Where do you come from, Mr. Haegeli?"

"Schaffhausen. You know Schaffhausen?" Mr. Haegeli asked.

"Yes, yes," I said in German. "*Wunderbar.*"

"*Ja, ja,* beautiful city."

"And the waterfall."

"You know the Haegeli Wurstfabrik there?"

"No. I'm sorry."

"Well, it's one of the biggest *Wurstfabriken* in Switzerland: liverwurst, salami, cervelat, frankfurters, boned hams —a big concern, belongs to a branch of my family. I'm a

sort of wanderer. I like to travel—restless, you know. I can't
see myself in Schaffhausen." He looked up. He was mixing
food with both hands, his arms rotating.

"I understand."

"Besides, we don't get along, my relatives and I. All they
think about is money, small money. I think in large sums.
I like a wide horizon. Schaffhausen is not for me."

"How long have you been traveling?"

"Oh, I'm now two years on this ship. You see, I'm not
really a butcher; I'm an inventor."

"How interesting! What are you working on, Mr. Haegeli?"

At last Mr. Haegeli turned his back on the cage in which
Little Bit waited. "Well, it's something tremendous. It's, so
to say, revolutionary."

"Oh!"

"There's a friend of mine, a Swiss, who is a baker, but, you
know, like I am no real butcher he is not exactly a baker.
I mean he knows his trade, but he has ambition to make
something of himself, and together we have created something that we call a Frankroll." He waited for the effect.

"What is a Frankroll?"

"It's a frankfurter baked inside a roll. We've got everything here to experiment with—the material and the ovens.
I make the franks, and he makes the roll. We've tried it out
on passengers here. Mr. Gruber, for example, says it's a
marvelous idea. I might add that the experimental stage is
over. Our product is perfect. And now it is merely a question of selling the patent or licensing somebody. You know
the way that is done; you make much more that way."

"Have you tried?"

Mr. Haegeli came close, the inventor's excitement in his

eyes now. "That is where the hitch comes in. On the last trip I saw the biggest frankfurter people in America; they're in New York. Well, the things you find out! They were very nice. The president received us, and he looked at the product and tasted it. He seemed to like it, because he called for his son and a man who works close to him. 'I think you've got something there,' the old man said. I think with him we would have had clear sailing, but he had one of these wisenheimers for a son."

As Haegeli talked, he completely forgot about his dogs. He gesticulated with his hands, which were sticky with hash, using them as a boxer does when he talks with his gloves on. Standing close to me, he held his hands away, lest dog food soil my clothes. He stood exactly right, with his back turned to Barbara as she slowly reached toward the door of Little Bit's cage.

It was all foiled again by the return of Mr. Gruber and Rolfi. Mr. Gruber kissed his dog good-night and watched him as he slowly walked into his cage. He said to Rolfi that it was only for two more nights that he had to be here. He wished us a good-night also, and after a final good-night to his dog he went.

"Where was I?" said the butcher.

"With the Frankroll, the old man, and the wise-guy son."

"Right. Well, the son was looking at our product doubtfully, and he took a bite out of it, and in the middle of it he stopped chewing. 'Mmmm,' he said, 'not bad, not bad at all. But—' He made a long pause, and then he said, 'What about the mustard, gentlemen?'

"I said, 'All right, what about the mustard?' So the wise guy says, 'I'm a customer; I'm buying; I'm at a hot-dog stand. I watch the man in the white jacket. He picks up the frankfurter roll that's been sliced and placed face down on the hot plate. Then he picks it up in a sanitary fashion, takes the skinless frank with his fork, places it on the roll, and hands it to me. Now I dip into the mustard pot, or maybe I decide on a little kraut, or maybe some relish. Anyway, I put all that on the frank—' He held out his hand.

"So I said, 'What's all that got to do with Frankroll?' So Junior says, 'A lot. Let me explain. It's got no appeal. Practical, maybe, but to put the mustard on the hot dog the customer would have to slice the bun first, and that leads us straight back to the old-fashioned roll. This may be practical, but it's got no sizzle to it. No eye appeal, no nose appeal. It's no good.'

"Well, the old man was confused, and he got up and said that he'd like.to think about it, and then he said he'd like to show us the factory. Well, you'd never think how important a thing a frankfurter is. This factory is shining. Now there are two schools about frankfurters, the skin frank and the skinless. These people specialize in skinless ones, because the American housewife is so lazy she prefers it without the skin. But did you know that the skinless comes with a skin that has to be peeled? Now there is a vast hall, and at long tables there sit hundreds of women, and music plays, and each has in her left hand a frankfurter and in the right a paring knife, and all day long they remove the skin from the frankfurters. An eight-hour day. And at the end of the room there is a first-aid station, because at the speed at which they work there is a great deal of laceration. The man there in charge—"

Barbara broke in, "Oh, please, Poppy, please!" she urged. "Let's get out of here."

"The man in charge there explained that in spite of elab-

orate safety precautions, there was a great deal of absen-
teeism on account of carelessness. They had people working
on a machine to skin the frankfurters. 'Now if you could
invent a skinning device,' said the old man to me, 'you'd
be a millionaire overnight.' Well, we're not licked yet. You
see, the beauty of working on a ship is you have everything.
One of the engineers is working with us on a skinning machine, and I have another outfit lined up for the Frankroll."

The light in Mr. Haegeli's eyes faded. He wiped his hand
again on his apron, and I shook it, and slowly Barbara and
I walked out on deck and down the first flight of stairs to
A deck, and I said, "Run for your life, for by now he has
discovered that Little Bit is gone."

We got into the cabin. Little Bit smiled on both sides of
his face, and he bounced from floor to bed and to chair.
There was a knock on the door. The thrill of the cops-and-
robbers game had begun. Little Bit had vanished.

"Who is it?" Barbara asked.

It was the steward. "Did you find him?"

Barbara smiled.

"You got him back?"

Barbara nodded. "Oh, for Heaven's sake, keep your dog
out of sight!" the steward said. "That crazy butcher is capa-
ble of anything from now on. I got a wife and family." The
steward was not one to bathe in the dark waters of con-
spiracy.

"From now on the dog must not be left," I said to Barbara.
"He must go with us wherever we go, to the dining room,
on deck, to the lounge, and to the movies. And you can't
carry him around in that bag; you'll have to cover him with
a scarf or have him inside your coat."

Barbara started going about as if her arm were in a sling.

The steward averted his eyes whenever he met us, and he didn't bring any more dog food.

Mr. Gruber said, "The kennelman suspects you of having removed the dog from the kennel."

"We did."

"Good," said the actor. "Anything I can do, I will."

"Well, act as if you didn't know anything about it. How is Rolfi?"

"Oh, Rolfi is fine. You know, he's never bitten anybody in his life except that kennelman."

Mr. Gruber offered to get Little Bit off the boat. He said he had a wicker basket in which he carried some of Rolfi's things, and he would empty that, except for Rolfi's coat, and in that he would carry Little Bit off the *America*, for the butcher would watch us closely—if he didn't find the dog before—and catch us at the customs.

"Isn't Mr. Gruber a nice man?" Barbara said. "People always say such mean things about movie actors."

Camouflaged in his scarf, Little Bit rested on Barbara's lap during meals. On the deck chair he lay motionless between my feet, covered by the steamer rug. He traveled about under Barbara's coat, and he took his exercise secretly on the afterdeck, while I watched from above.

After the morning walk the next day, the steward knocked, and he looked worried. "The butcher was here," he said, "and he went all over the room. He found the dish with *Always Faithful* on it on the bathroom floor."

"How could we be so careless?" I said, my pride hurt.

"And of course he saw the bag with Little Bit printed on it. I said I didn't know nothing about a dog."

We doubled our precautions. Little Bit's mouth was down

at the edges with worry. I contemplated what to do. After all, there was only one more day, and if the worst happened we could sit upstairs near the kennel with Little Bit, the way Mr. Gruber sat with Rolfi.

I said to Barbara, "Perhaps it would be best to pay the passage and have it over with."

"No, you can't do that. Think of the poor steward and his family."

"Well, we could settle that, I think, with the butcher anyway. I don't like to cheat the line."

"Well, Poppy, you can send them a check after, if that worries you, or drink a few bottles of champagne, or buy something in the shop."

There was a knock on the door.

"Who is it?"

"The purser, sir."

"Please come in."

The door opened, and outside behind the purser stood Mr. Haegeli.

"Just wanted to look and see if everything was all right," the purser said. "Are you comfortable, sir? Anything I can do?"

"Everything is fine."

"By the way, sir," the purser went on, "we are looking for a small white dog that's been lost. We wondered if by any chance it is in here."

"Come in. Look for yourself," I said.

"That's quite all right, sir. Excuse the intrusion. Good evening." The purser closed the door.

"What a nice man!" said Barbara.

The butcher was excluded from pursuing us in the public

rooms of the ship. He couldn't follow us to the movies or the dining room. But he seemed to have spies.

"What a lovely scarf you have there, miss!" said the elevator boy, and after that we used the stairs.

The butcher came on deck and followed us on the evening promenade around the deck, while Little Bit sat inside my overcoat and I held him in place with my right hand in a Napoleonlike pose. We made four turns around deck. We saw the butcher's shadow on the wall near the stairs several times. He seemed to be nearing a nervous breakdown. Mr. Gruber told us that he had sworn we had the dog and that he meant to find it at any cost. There was one more night to go, and the next day the ship would dock.

At ten Barbara would deliver Little Bit to Mr. Gruber, and we would fill the bag in which he traveled with paper handkerchiefs, tobacco, soap, extra toothbrushes, razor blades, dental floss, and other things, all of which can be had in Europe but which, for some droll reason, one always takes along.

Little Bit was fed from luncheon trays that we ordered for ourselves in the cabin instead of going down to lunch.

The steward was shaking. "I don't know when that guy takes care of the other dogs," he said. "He's hanging around here all the time. I hope you'll get off all right."

It was the last night on board. The sun had set again, and we came up on the promenade deck to take the evening walk. The butcher was there, following us. He walked faster than usual. It was cold and windy. I went inside with Barbara and drank a cocktail in the bar, and Barbara, with her lemonade in her hand, suddenly said, "He's watching us through the third window."

I looked quickly toward the left side of the room; the

butcher's face was pressed against the glass, pale and haunting.

He kept watch from the outside and ran back and forth as we moved about inside.

We went to the dining room. When we came back I got a cigar, and he was outside the bar. When I went to the saloon to have coffee, he was outside the window.

"Don't give Little Bit any sugar," Barbara said. "He's watching us."

Busboys were clearing the floor for dancing, and we got up to walk back to the library. There is a windowless passage between the main saloon and the library, and off this passage is the gift shop. On this last evening people stood there in numbers buying cigarettes, film, small sailor hats, miniature life belts, and ship models with SS *America* written on them. Here I suddenly conceived the miraculous solution of our problem. It was in front of me on a shelf. Among an assortment of toy animals, stuffed Mickey Mice, Donald Ducks, and Teddy bears of various sizes stood the exact replica of Little Bit—the same button eyes, patent-leather nose, the fluff, the sticklike legs, the pompon at the end of the tail, and a red ribbon in its hair.

"How much is that dog?" I asked the young lady.

"It's two ninety-five, sir," she replied.

"I'll take it."

"Shall I wrap it up, sir?"

"No, thanks. I'll take it as is."

"What are we going to do now, Poppy?"

"Now you keep Little Bit hidden, and I'll take the stuffed dog, and we'll go into the library."

We sat down, and I placed the stuffed dog at my side and spoke to it. The butcher was on the far side of the ship, but he almost went through the window. Then he disappeared and ran around to the other side. I had arranged it so that the dog seemed to be sleeping at my side, partly covered by Barbara's scarf. I told her to take Little Bit down to the cabin and then to come back.

When she came back, Barbara took the toy dog and fixed its hair and combed the fluff, and then I said, "Please give me the dog." We walked the length of the ship on the inside. The butcher was sprinting outside, his face appearing flashlike in a series of windows.

At the front of the ship we went out on deck, and I held the dog so that the white pompon stuck out in back, and I wiggled it a little to give it the illusion of life. It took the butcher a while to catch up. He walked fast; we walked faster. He almost ran; we ran. He shouted, "Mister!"

I continued running, and as we approached the stern, I said, "Can you let out a terrible scream?"

"Yes, of course," said Barbara.

"One, two, three—now."

As she screamed, we got to the end of the ship. I threw the dog in a wide curve into the sea.

The butcher, only a few feet away, gripped the railing and looked below, where the small white form bobbed up and down in the turbulent water and was rapidly washed away in the wake of the *America*.

I turned to go back into the saloon.

We left the butcher paralyzed at the stern of the *America*. He was not at the gangplank the next day, and on the return trip there was another man in charge of the kennels.

The Long Duel *Robert Murphy*

It was the dog that brought Yancy back into Jake Fisher's mind again after so many years: Yancy the debonair, the intrepid, cool hunter, who had once stood up to a bear with nothing but a knife to prove to himself that he wasn't afraid of fear, the man Jake had so tremendously admired. For Jake had been victimized by an overactive imaginative in those youthful days and afraid of many things; it was natural that Yancy had become a hero to him, that he had struggled desperately to impose Yancy's code upon himself.

This had been one of the things that formed him; it had never gone out of his life, but the quiet uneventfulness of

59

the intervening years had pushed it back into his subconscious. He surely wasn't thinking about it as he rode home from jury duty in Mountain City, but every step the horse took brought Yancy and a boyhood fear closer to him again.

Jake had no intimation of this as he rode along the twisting, rocky trail with his collar turned up against the afternoon chill in the mountain air. He wasn't paying much attention to the horse, which had been bred in the Great Smokies and knew its way well enough. His strong, stocky body functioned with unconscious and sympathetic skill to ease the horse, and his broad, darkly pleasant face, with its tanned cheeks and candid brown eyes, was preoccupied. He was thinking of what the lawyer from Elizabethton had said when court was over, the lawyer's talk about wild boars.

Somebody from North Carolina had imported a couple of them from the Harz Mountains back in 1912, the lawyer said, and they had interbred with wild hogs; the progeny of these matings had crossed the mountains into Tennessee. They were as fierce and strong as any animal in the world, the lawyer said, mean as the devil and quick as snakes. They'd charge a man without provocation and rip him up, and sports from Chattanooga came up in November and hunted them with Platt hounds. The Platt hounds were a strain of Airedale.

One of these boars had killed a man in the Unaka Mountains around Christmastime, a fine hunter who'd had two of these Platt hounds. The hunter got into a corner apparently, and the boar had got him and one of the hounds. Nobody knew where the other hound had gone. It never came home, and nobody found it anywhere.

Jake had been interested in the story, because he'd never known before that boars were in the state and because they awakened in him the memories of his most devastating boyhood fear. His grandfather, a genial, bearded old wood-carver from the Harz Mountains, had pictured them as more dangerous than tigers—great four-hundred-pound brutes with six-inch tusks, lying malignantly in wait for hunters in the gloomy Prussian forests, peering out of the shadows with their evil little pig eyes.

The involuntary shiver accompanying these youthful imaginings came back to him again as he recalled the lawyer's talk. Then the horse stopped abruptly with a snort, almost pitching Jake over its head.

He clawed his way back into the saddle, staring between the horse's erect ears. An animal had emerged from the shadows about forty feet ahead and stood facing him. He had been so preoccupied with boars that he thought for an instant he was looking at one of them.

The hair on his neck stirred, and his mind searched frantically for a way of getting the horse off the trail if it charged. Then he saw that it wasn't a boar, but a dog. He kicked the horse and moved forward. The dog looked like an Airedale; it had a rough tan-and-black coat. It stood in the path, watching quietly, neither friendly nor unfriendly, with such a withdrawn, self-sufficient quality about it that Jake's curiosity was aroused, for no dog would be on that lonely mountain unless it was lost, and lost dogs were usually pathetically glad to see anyone.

"Hello!" Jake said, and grinned. He had a disarming grin that bunched his cheeks and crinkled the corners of his eyes. "Hello, fellow!"

The dog wagged his tail slightly but made no advances.

He slid off the horse and, walking to the dog, ran his square, strong fingers along its spine and around the bases of its ears. It was very thin; the rough coat was stretched over the ribs, but the muscles were hard and tight. It accepted the handling as it had accepted his greeting, undemonstratively. Jake's fingers caught in the thin collar concealed by the rough coat, and he turned it until the brass plate came up. The plate was engraved:

> *Rouse*
> *A. Yancy*
> *Elm Mills*
> *Tenn.*

Jake straightened up quickly and stared at the dog. All his memories of Yancy came back to him again, bringing a sense of protest, a poignant sense of loss. He realized instantly that this was the dog the lawyer had talked about, the dog that had vanished after its master had been killed by the boar. It was as if something fine, something very necessary to him, had suddenly gone out of his life. It was almost impossible for him to believe Yancy was not invincible; the boar must have caught him unaware. And as this thought came into Jake's mind he began to hate the boar. He had never had cause to hate an animal before.

Confused by this new emotion, he continued to stare at the dog, and as he stared at it wonder came into his mind. What was it doing here, fifty miles from the scene of Yancy's death, hard miles in a mountain country where some of the peaks ran up over five thousand feet? The fight had occurred six months ago. Where had the dog sheltered during the bitter mountain winter? Was it so grieved by Yancy's death that it had become a wanderer, mourning for him? That it had traveled widely was evident from its muscles; that it had managed to survive at all was an unbelievable thing.

Jake bent over it with closer attention. There was a long scar, nearly healed now, along its left side. The boar must have done that, must have scored with those terrible six-inch tusks.

Thinking of its loyalty and its loneliness, feeling his own sense of loss, Jake wanted the dog. He wanted it more than the three he had at home: Bella, the Virginia shepherd, or the two coon hounds, Music and Plunger. They were good dogs, but not one of them could have gone on in loneliness and privation as this dog had done; not one of them was connected with the memories this dog invoked. He'd take it home. "Rouse!" he said. "Rouse!"

The dog raised its head quickly and looked at him, its ear pricked. Its eyes were attentive and questioning, but it seemed to look beyond him, waiting, as though expecting the familiar syllable to be spoken by another voice. Jake mounted, walked the horse a few steps, and turned. Rouse hadn't moved. He was standing beside the trail looking after Jake, waiting and attentive.

"Rouse!" Jake called. "Rouse!"

The dog's docked tail wagged slightly. For a moment he stood there, a lonely figure against the thicket's dark shadows, then turned and trotted from the trail. Jake called his name again urgently and whistled, but he didn't reappear. Far off in the undergrowth a twig cracked, and then silence fell. Regretfully, Jake rode on.

* * *

In the deep, narrow little valley where Jake's farm lay, things fell back into their accustomed routine. The hired man, Rufe—a lanky, drawling mountain man—had carried things on and there was no back work. Jake worked the corn and the vegetable patches with Rufe, sent Bella out to drive in the two cows at milking time, and spent the short evenings reading and carving little figures before the fire with the three dogs around him. Isolated as he was, he had a lonely, quiet life, which suited him. He had a little money, kept his place neatly, and fared better than the few families round about. He would have been happy if he hadn't encountered Rouse.

The remembrance of the dog standing lonely and waiting in the trail stayed with him, that and the sense of loss over Yancy's death. Yancy became real to him once more, and thinking so much of Yancy, of the empty place left by Yancy's death, Jake wanted the dog increasingly. It would have been a link with the past, and he was sure it had wanted to come with him. The expression of its eyes indicated plainly that it knew well enough what it was giving up.

He knew the dog liked him; they all liked him. They seemed to understand at once the kindliness of his square, strong hands and of his sentimental German heart, to accept him without reservations. He fulfilled their need of warmth and affection, the ancient heritage of their domesticity. No dog had ever refused to follow him before. It was, in a way, an indication of their softness, an indication that their need of affection was the greatest thing in their lives. The fact that Rouse was not bound by this, that he had set out upon a lonely and sorrowful odyssey, gave him a striking individuality and set him apart, made him a dog worthy of Yancy.

Jake couldn't get the dog out of his mind. He would sit thinking about him, staring into the fire with his pipe or a half-finished carving in his hand, until the outraged Bella would get up from her rug and thrust her head into his lap.

There came an afternoon when Jake, busy in his little shop behind the barn, looked up and realized that dusk was beginning to fall. He wondered why Bella wasn't back. He had sent her after the cows, and she was always back before the light began to fail, barking in the yard to let them know the cows were ready to be milked.

He put the chisel back into the rack and went outside. The cows were standing uneasily in the yard, but Bella was nowhere in sight. For the first time Jake thought of the boar. A sudden, tense uneasiness took hold of him, and he ran into the house. Rufe, with the two hounds near him, was washing in the kitchen and raised his dripping face questioningly.

"Bella," Jake said. "Where's Bella?"

Jake, grabbing the rifle from the corner, interrupted him. "Keep the hounds here," he said, and, jamming a cartridge into the rifle, ran out. He could hear the hounds' sudden uproar of excitement as he ran.

The cows trotted off a few yards and stared stupidly at him as he went past them. He finally pulled up, panting at the edge of the pasture. It was a triangular piece of land, narrowing before him to its apex between the steep sides of the ridge, broken by clumps of willow and birch.

Shadows were deepening over it, but off to the left, among
the darkening tangle, his eye caught a faint gleam of white.

"Bella!" he shouted. "Bella!"

The white spot didn't move. But before the echo of his
voice died out, the boar moved in the cover and vanished
again, a great, dark beast frosted with gray, with a head
nearly as large as its body. The tusks gleamed for an instant in the gloom, and then it was gone.

He made a step to go after it, but something inside him
tightened up and stopped him. It was dark in there, dark
and thick; in the darkness the brute that had been too
much for Yancy waited. The memories of his grandfather's
tales moved obscurely in his mind, and his legs refused to
move. He couldn't go on. He stood waiting for the boar to
go away, knowing what he would find. Bella had been a
splendid bitch of a local breed, affectionate and trust-
worthy, too unsuspicious and accustomed to the ways of
domestic cattle and swine for the sudden, slashing ferocity
of the boar.

He went back to the house and picked up the old hooked
rug on which she had slept. Rufe put the hounds in the
kitchen and went back with him without speaking. In
silence they wrapped Bella's body in the rug and buried
her where the boar had killed her.

It was dark when they returned to the barn and got
the cows milked and bedded down, and the hounds had
fallen quiet. They didn't talk about it even then. Rufe
muttered a subdued, "Night," and went to bed early. Jake
spent the evening before the fire. Once or twice he looked
up from it to see where Bella was.

Slow rage began to burn within him. He finally went to
bed, but he couldn't sleep; as he tossed about, his rage

increased. The hate he had felt for the boar upon learning of Yancy's death had been an abstract emotion, for hate was alien to him. Further, he had been preoccupied with thoughts of Yancy and Rouse. Now that the boar had ap-appeared, however, the rage was abstract no longer, and Bella's death had intensified it.

He clenched his fists beneath the blankets, wanting to kill the boar, to do away with it for its senseless ferocity in taking Yancy and Bella away from him. He recalled his unwillingness at the pasture's edge, but as his rage increased he excused himself for it. It would have been foolhardy, he thought, to go into the dark thicket. Daylight was the time to deal with a brute like that, and in the morning he'd deal with it. Under this determination something very like fear lurked, but he had worked himself past the point of seeing it.

Early in the morning Rufe found him making sandwiches by lamplight. Rufe, as was his custom, asked no questions, but he stood by so obviously expecting an explanation that Jake finally said, "It was a boar killed Bella. I'm going after it."

"A boar?" Rufe asked, and rubbed his long chin. "I ain't seen nary a boar ever, but I hear tell they's pow'ful mean. I reckon I'll go along."

Jake shook his dark head. "No," he said. "You stay here."

"Likely you'll need help. I reckon I'll go."

"No," Jake said. Although he tried to control his voice, it took a faint edge of irritation.

Rufe gave in. "Sure," he said. "Only don't you mess with no rifle. You take the gun. Likely you'll come up with him in a thick place, where the shootin's close and quick. You mind out, Jake. You mind out. I ain't likin' no boars."

Jake agreed, dismissed him to his work, locked the hounds in the kitchen, and started out. He went first to the pasture, back into the thickets where the boar had been. Its tracks were easily followed for a way, but he lost them on higher ground. Then he recalled his grandfather saying that boars in the old country usually hid in the daytime and moved about at dusk and dawn. After that, he stayed close to thicker cover, along the streams and near boggy places.

He hunted slowly and carefully, in a cold rage. He was always in the shadows, and after a while it became touchy work. His imagination began to overcome his rage, and by noon his nerves were playing him tricks. For each gloomy thicket he drew blank the tension increased. The realization that the boar had been too much for Yancy came closer all the time. The expectation built up that the next thicket would bring the boar down on him, in a place too thick to swing the gun.

It was nearly noon by the sun when he decided to quit. He had worked into another narrow little valley, and it was swampy and thick. He didn't like the look of it from the first, but he went into it. The shadows fell cool and deep, and when a rabbit burst from its squat with a great rattle of twigs, his heart leaped up with it. He hesitated, then decided to go to the end of the thicket. The shadows grew more secretive and menacing.

He could never remember, afterward, the start of the boar's charge. One moment was held by brooding silence, the next filled the world with crashing pandemonium. The gun leaped up, caught a branch, and was torn from his hands. The next instant the black bulk was upon him. Its size was far beyond his expectations, and it moved with unbelievable speed.

He had one swift impression of the great ugly head with its gleaming tusks and leaped sideways. There was a blow —a mighty hand to which his weight was nothing seemed to catch at his leg, spin him into the air, and hurl him down. He scrambled up desperately, caught a limb, and swung himself clear as the boar charged again. It raged about below as he pulled his legs up and flattened on a limb, making short, vicious rushes, gashing great splinters from the trunk, squealing and gnashing jaws slobbered with foam.

In quickness and malevolent power it was even worse than his grandfather had claimed; it was truly a devil come out of his boyhood. It held him there for nearly an hour, charging about and looking wickedly up at him, then went reluctantly off. Only then did he discover that one leg of his heavy corduroys had been cleanly slit from cuff to knee and the skin of his leg beneath it left with a long red welt.

An uncontrollable nervous trembling seized him as he stared at it. The charge had been a near thing, a moment of pure, blind terror, and he knew he couldn't face another one. It wasn't the fear of death that brought him to this. He had faced death calmly several times; there was plenty of courage in his stocky body. It was a fear of the boar, an uncontrollable and violent revulsion of his nerves latent in him since boyhood, an irresistible revolt against a certain object, just as another man's nerves would have revolted against a snake.

He realized that his nerves and not his mind had tricked him, that he had been beaten before he went into the thicket. He had let the killer of Yancy and Bella escape, but the thing that stabbed him was his failure to dominate himself. The code he had built upon Yancy had failed, and in failing he had let Yancy down. Sentimental in most things, he was not sentimental in this; there was a very bitter taste in his mouth.

Now that his fear was fully revealed, Jake didn't try to justify it again. There was too much forthright honesty in him for that. It was there and he couldn't escape it. Neither could he bear to live with it. He considered endless expedients for killing the boar, but could hit upon nothing practical. He fretted over it until his mind, as a defense measure, swung him into the belief that the boar had moved on and wouldn't come to the farm again, that it was beyond his reach in the wilderness surrounding him.

This was a poor escape and he half realized it. He was silent and unhappy. For three days he worked alone with the hounds near him and the rifle handy, and his bitterness at himself mounted. On the third afternoon he was walking from the barn to the house, the hounds beside him, when they suddenly leaped, growling, toward the porch. He looked up, yelling at them, and saw Rouse standing by the steps. He was too surprised to yell again.

Rouse stood still, and the hounds bore down on him. He was an interloper, a stranger, and the hounds intended to drive him off. They made for him together, and he didn't move until they were almost upon him. By that time Jake had gathered his wits sufficiently to yell again. He wanted Rouse desperately, and he thought that Rouse, like most dogs so attacked in a strange place, would turn tail and be lost to him. He yelled with all the strength of his lungs, but it was too late to stop the hounds. They leaped in, and instead of running Rouse sidestepped with flashing quickness, rolled Plunger over by a shoulder blow, and slashed Music.

While Jake ran for them the fight practically settled itself. Rouse was everywhere at once, slashing them both, bounding between them with a swift and expert coolness that left them snapping empty air. They were seasoned fighters, but by the time Jake ran up they'd had enough and were ready to be called off. He put them into the house, came out again, sat down on the step, and called Rouse to him.

Rouse came and stood before him quietly but withdrawn, accepting the hands that stroked his head. Lonely and depressed, Jake at first stroked him without thought, soothed by the dog's presence and association with Yancy. But as the rhythmic play of his fingers continued a sort of confidence seemed to enter them from the clean, hard skull, a feeling that the dog would help him vanquish his fear. As this hope was born in Jake he began to talk to the dog softly and ingratiatingly. His hands, shrewd in their knowledge of nerve centers, played more widely over the dog in an effort to bind it to him.

As he rubbed the harsh coat he noticed the scar again. It was all but healed, and as he looked at it he realized that it had healed more during the short time since he had seen the dog than it had during the entire winter. He puzzled over that for a moment. Suddenly it came to him: Rouse hadn't got the scar when Yancy died. He had got it after that, much later. Rouse's wanderings weren't from grief; they had a grim purpose. Ever since Yancy's death Rouse had trailed the boar, forever seeking and fighting it, hounding it implacably, determined to run it down.

Jake stopped rubbing and stared at the dog, his imagination caught by the spirit of Nemesis in the thin, iron-
muscled body. In his mind's eye he saw Rouse wandering
through the freezing cold and snow of winter, the fogs and
raw winds of spring, lonely and starving, blind to suffering
and fear, terribly outclassed by the boar, but never giving
in. The odds were all against him, yet he had kept on fighting a desperate guerrilla warfare of ambush and swift attack and flight. Again and again it had happened: the dash
in the shadows, the squealing, murderous charge, the frantic work.

Such iron courage shamed him by making him realize
his own evasions, but it brought him hope as well, hope
that the dog's example, like Yancy's so long ago, would aid
him in defeating his traitorous nerves. The saving warmth
of this hope leaped up in him. He ran into the house, returned with a heaping plate of meat, and watched Rouse
eat. When the dog had finished, he called it into the house.
It entered quietly and stayed near him; the hounds
bristled, but kept their distance.

Rufe came in and accepted Rouse as he had accepted
the first hunt for the boar. He knew Jake would tell the
whole story when he felt like it. Jake talked to Rouse
while the supper was cooked and eaten. When he lit the
fire and sat down before it, Rouse lay down on the small
rug before the hearth, watched him for a while, and went
to sleep. He slept profoundly, but even in sleep he remained a little remote, a visitor who appreciated hospital-
ity but withheld allegiance.

Jake smoked and watched him, more at peace than he
had been for days, the hope warm within him. He was sure
that now he had Rouse inside, warmed and fed and com-

fortable, he would be able to keep him. When he was sure of the dog, they could start out together. The fire died down and he got up. Rouse got up too and going to the door scratched upon it.

"No," Jake said. "You'd better stay inside tonight."

Rouse whined from the door, and Jake walked over to him. Outside, the moon was full. The barn and the little valley were overlaid with calm silver, and beyond them the ridge rose sharp and black into the luminous sky. Rouse whined and thrust an ingratiating moist nose into his hand.

"No, no, old fellow," Jake said. "I need you here." He went into the bedroom. Rouse followed, moving restlessly about, and finally Jake took him into the living room. "Lie down," he said. Rouse went to the hearthrug, but remained standing as Jake closed the bedroom door.

Jake got into bed. He heard Rouse come to his door and whine once more. "Go to bed, Rouse," he said quietly and kindly.

The dog moved about for a short while; then there was the quick patter of feet and a crash. The hounds bayed. Jake jumped out of bed and ran into the living room. Rouse wasn't there, and the window overlooking the porch was broken. Jake ran to the door and pulled it open, but Rouse had gone.

Jake came back into the living room and kicked up the fire. He didn't sit down. He rested one hand on the mantel he'd carved himself and stood perfectly still, highlighted softly by the flames. For a while there was only one thought in his head: Rouse, with the strange prescience of animals, had sensed the fear in him, had realized that if he stayed Jake would gradually give up the determination to go after the boar. This thought may have been fantastic or it may have been true. Jake was in no emotional state to analyze it; the saving thing was that it brought to him a shame more unbearable than his fear.

His mind became full of pictures of Rouse and Rouse's courageous and hopeless struggles with the boar. And beneath all this, he knew the boar would be back. Someday it would come out of the shadows to attack the cows or Rufe or himself. He stood there with his belly going hollow and cold within him and he knew that he would have to face the boar alone.

Once more Rufe entered the lamplit kitchen as he was making up his pack and stood silently by. He looked up. Rufe's eyes were on him solemnly; his long face expressed concern. Jake, tired by the emotions of the night, and apprehensive, suddenly felt grateful to him for his silent and unobtrusive sympathy. "I'm going after him again, Rufe," he said. "I can't let him run me off my own place."

Rufe nodded. "I figgered you was studying on it," he said. "I reckon this time I ain't stayin' here."

"Yes," Jake said. "I'd like you to stay here this time too."

Rufe's long jaw set. "It's right discomfortable stayin' here. I ain't such a weaklin' in a scuffle."

"You're a good man anywhere," Jake said, "but I have to settle this myself." He forestalled Rufe's protest. "Have you ever been afraid of anything, Rufe?"

"I reckon," Rufe said. "Back to home, I was scared of Lije Harkness. He pestered me, and I was pow'ful scared of him. I was always studying to git my kin and tromple him."

"And what did you do?"

Rufe grinned sheepishly. "Come a day, I rose and

trompled him myself. I was too scared not to tromple him."

"It's the same thing," Jake said. His brown eyes pleaded for Rufe to make it easier. "You see why you can't go."

Rufe considered, long and heavily. "I reckon," he said. Then he added hopefully, "Only, this hog ain't no Harkness. Harknesses come clean out in the open when they lay for you." He glanced at Jake to see if this ingenuous by-path should be followed up and saw that it shouldn't. "Well," he said with resignation, "I got work outside. I shore wish you luck, Jake. You git that dog. Can you find him?"

Jake nodded. They shook hands without speaking again, their hands gripping hard, and Rufe went out. As Jake pulled the straps tight on his pack Music, unable to keep still longer, came wiggling over to him.

"You can go," Jake said. "You've got to go this time. And maybe you won't come back. Lie down now."

Music returned to his place. Jake got into his denim coat, eased the pack onto his back, and took a long look around the familiar room. He got the gun and a pocketful of buckshot shells, tied Music to his belt with a ten-foot length of cord, picked up the rug on which Rouse had slept, and went outside. The hounds scrambled excitedly about, but he called them and made them sniff the rug.

"Find dog!" he ordered. "Find dog!" The hounds lost some of their enthusiasm and looked at him unhappily. He knew he would have trouble holding them to Rouse's scent, but it could be done. "Find dog!" he ordered again.

They went out past the barn and through the pasture, then began to work up the ridge. At first Jake was very jumpy, but as the outlines of leaves overhead strengthened against the paling sky and the details of rocks and deadfall

timber emerged from the general monotone of the ground
a sort of detachment came on him. There was a penetrating
chill in the air, and the woods were dripping wet. Music
constantly entangled his rope in the underbrush, and
Plunger worked too far ahead and had to be called in frequently.

Jake was afraid to let Music off the rope for fear both
hounds would get too far ahead and be lost; he endured
the tugging and entanglements patiently. By the time the
sun was up his detachment had deepened into a sort of
numbness that went all through him and even immobilized
thought. Only his nerves were alive.

By early afternoon his muscles were aching. He had been
climbing stiff ridges or sliding down them since sunrise
with his nerves at an increasing tensity, and the constant
pull of Music at his belt hadn't helped. The hounds were
tiring too; it was increasingly difficult to control them. But
he went on and presently came out into a small glade with
a tumbling stream on the edge of it.

The grass had been torn up and the bushes flattened, and
as Jake searched around he found a few spots of dried
blood on a gray rock and the footprints of both dog and
boar. His hands began to tremble, and he endeavored to
get the hounds on Rouse's scent. Their hackles rose as they
sniffed about, but otherwise they refused to take any interest. They'd had enough of it; they looked at him mourn-
fully, sat down, and ran their tongues out.

Jake cursed them wanly and set out again. The cold hol-
lowness returned to his belly, and suddenly, against the
late-afternoon stillness of the woods in which even the
leaves hung motionless, his heart began to pound in his ears.

They came to another opening, a parklike place surrounded by small maples. Plunger was trotting twenty feet ahead when suddenly he stiffened and snarled. There was a crash of underbrush, and Jake didn't have time for fear, for any conscious thought whatever. The boar burst out of the maples and came for him head down, like a black projectile. Plunger leaped aside, and the boar, turning with the sudden, lunging quickness of all swine, made for Music. Jake fired, Music dodged with a yank on the cord that ruined his aim, and the boar went between them, cutting the cord.

The boar wheeled and came for Jake. Both hounds closed in on it, and Plunger was tossed into the air. Jake fired the other barrel. The boar fell forward and leaped up again. It started to squeal. Music fastened on its hind leg, but it whirled and tossed Music too and came again for Jake.

Although Jake might have had time to reload the gun, he never thought of it. For an instant he stood there frozen, staring at the squealing boar. He saw in violent motion the heavy, bristled shoulders and the gleaming tusks, the evil little eyes, and the terror of it rushed over him.

The overwhelming urge to avoid it, the nerves' blind panic, held him powerless, and as he stared something happened to his sense of time. The swift action became slowed and prolonged, like the action in a dream. There was a long moment when his courage went out to meet the boar, unfaltering and bright, and he recognized the courage and was glad of it.

And then, from beyond his field of vision, Rouse appeared and tore the boar's hindquarters. The boar squealed on a higher note. He saw it turn with an upward sweep of the tusks, but Rouse leaped clear as a salmon leaps clear of a wave. Twisting and beautifully coordinated, he sidestepped another charge, sank his teeth in the boar, and leaped aside. But he didn't leap away; he closed once more and the boar tossed him, but even then he didn't retreat. He twisted in the air and recovered his balance, feinted and attacked. Then Jake knew that the old guerrilla tactics were done with. Rouse had heard the gun; he knew that Jake was somewhere near and counted on him and would fight until he came.

Safe now to climb a maple and escape, Jake knew what the finish would be. Foreseeing the death of the dog because it knew only Yancy's courage, he was lifted above the spell that his nerves had imposed upon his mind. His mind commanded once more. He jammed two shells into the gun, and with the loathing and terror of the boar rising in him like a physical sickness he ran toward it.

Rouse spun into the air, and the boar stepped back squealing, throwing its head up to rend him as he fell. The bloody foam of its paws was flung over Jake, and its mad eyes rolled toward him. Against the defeated and intolerable protest of his nerves he ran closer to it and fired both barrels into its head. Its legs collapsed and it fell. Rouse dropped a short distance away, whipped about, and fastened upon it. But it never moved again, and Rouse relinquished his hold and stood looking at Jake.

Jake stared back at him. The hounds came up, but Jake was only dimly aware of them. He knew that he was worthy of Yancy at last, that the code he had built upon Yancy was safe forever. A great feeling of triumph was born in him.

"Rouse!" he said. "Rouse!"

The dog looked once more at his dead enemy, then came toward Jake. His side was raked and bleeding, and he limped, but his eyes had lost entirely their expression of questioning and remoteness.

Jake bent down. His hands reached out to rub the harsh coat along the spine, but Rouse forestalled him. He put his head on Jake's lowered shoulder and licked Jake's ear with a quick, warm urgency. They stayed that way for a moment, and when Jake straightened up and walked away from the dead boar, Rouse walked beside him, his head under Jake's hand.

He knows, Jake thought. He's sure now. Maybe, before, he could feel that I was afraid. That's over, and he'll never go away again. And Yancy knows too. He's Yancy's and mine.

His fingers touched the clean, narrow terrier skull, and the sense of triumph came over him more keenly than before.

The Red Dog
Howard Maier

This is the story of a dog, an Irish setter named Spook.
In him flowed the blood of an ancient line; his regality was
evident in the grace with which he carried himself, in the
lift of his head, the dignity of his step, and in his deep-red
mahogany coat. From the tip of his sensitive nose to the
feathery sword of his tail, he was a king—a king who ruled
me with the gentle power of love.

When war came, Spook was my most serious problem.
The Army would take care of me, but who would take care
of Spook? For weeks I wrestled with the problem and could
find no solution. In desperation—for it was almost time to

go—I put the setter in the car and drove to a little town upstate where I spent my summers. The owner of the local garage was an old friend of mine with whom I had often hunted.

Would he take Spook? No strings attached? (The war had just begun, and who had the courage to forecast his own return from it?) I was giving him my dog, and with dogs one cannot give and then take back. But would he hunt him? Would he take good care of him? And, most important of all and impossible to put into words, would he love him?

Yes, my friend said, he would take him and hunt him and care for him. But he said nothing about love, for though men may write this word, they rarely use it. I watched as he patted the dog's head and the hand was gentle, and Spook thumped the floor with his tail, but his eyes remained fixed on my face.

All the way up in the car he had watched me instead of hanging half out the window in his customary manner. A dog senses many things besides game. Without another word, I handed my friend the lead and got into my car and drove away; even today I cannot truly remember whether I heard Spook bark or only imagined it. Generally, I am a slow and careful driver, but that day I drove for ten miles at top speed before slowing down.

After a month in the Army I wrote my friend a letter inquiring after the dog. I received no reply. Each camp was farther afield, and from each camp I wrote a letter. No answer ever came. I began to write to other friends in the village and in each letter I asked for news of my dog. Some of them answered, but of those that did none spoke of the dog. Spook is dead, I thought. He must be, otherwise they would answer. Rather than face the actuality of it, I gave up making inquiries and tried my best to put the dog from my mind.

Four years passed; the war was over. I had married, and my wife and I lived in the city. Summer was here, and we had taken a small house in the upstate village for our vacation. As we packed the bags in the car, Laurette suddenly looked up and said, "Suppose we run into your Spook—?"

"Spook is dead," I said shortly, and she took one look at my face and never finished her question.

The minute we arrived at the village I drove to the garage, although the tank was still half full. I left Laurette in the car and went into the office. My friend greeted me as if only a weekend had intervened since our last meeting, as if there had been no war, as if there had never been a question of a dog between us. Finally I couldn't stand it any longer and blurted out, "What happened to Spook?"

"Why nothing happened to him," my friend said. "He's as hale and hearty as you or I. I saw him only the other day."

My relief was so sharp that there was no room for anger. Bewildered, I said, "What do you mean you saw him? Don't you have him anymore?"

At that he had the grace to look shamefaced. He said, "I was drafted, and I didn't know I was going to be turned down, so I gave him away—to a minister, lives up above Willow."

"Why didn't you answer my letters?"

His face flushed with embarrassment. "I'm no hand at writing," he said. "Don't think I've written a letter in ten years."

I stared at him. Was it possible that he, having read my letters pleading for news of the dog, didn't realize what Spook meant to me?

The fact that he didn't was written on his honest, embarrassed face. He was country bred; to him a dog was an animal. It slept outdoors with the other animals, and when fall came it was hunted, and that was all.

"What's the name of the minister?" I asked him.

"Oh, Spook's not with him anymore. To tell the truth, he's had five, maybe six masters since then. Lives up with some summer people named Croker now, up past Shady. But we all see him. He visits around, makes plenty of stops. He's a valley dog now."

"A valley dog?"

"On his own. Cruises back and forth. Twenty miles one way or the other's nothing to him. Perfect condition, hard as nails. In the fall a man goes out with a gun, and there's Spook ready and willing to tag along."

There was nothing to say; it was obvious that he thought the life of a valley dog the best possible life any dog could have.

"Sorry about the letters," he said, still ashamed.

"It's all right," I said. I paid for my gas and went out to the car. I drove the mile to the house without saying anything. All the way, Laurette kept looking at me. When we turned into the drive, she said gently, "Spook's alive, isn't he?"

I nodded my head, and we let it go at that. After dinner I told her the whole story, and she let me tell it without asking any questions. At the end, she asked, "Are you going to try to see him?"

"Well, sure," I said. "Why not?"

"I wouldn't," Laurette said. "It would only hurt you, and it would hurt him more. Don't try to find him. It sounds as if he's very happy now."

"Don't be silly. Do you think he'd remember me? After four years and six masters?"

She just looked at me, and that was the end of the discussion. Two weeks passed; we worked and went swimming and lay around, and we never talked about the dog.

Then one day I saw Spook.

During a climb up the side of the valley I had stopped to rest on a rock that overlooked an open pasture in the woods beneath me. A boy of about sixteen came out of the trees, and then a second later Spook raced out into the sunlight. I knew him at once. I would have known Spook anywhere.

The boy walked straight across the pasture, but Spook, as was his habit, quartered the field, racing far ahead, then back again. And all the time the sun was glancing from his coat as if from a shield of burnished copper. I had seldom seen him look so well or so beautiful. It took them about three minutes to cross the field, then the trees on the far side swallowed them both. The pasture had never been so empty.

When I returned to the house I told Laurette about it. She said, "Away up there on the side of the hill? How could you know it was Spook?"

"How do I know you're you?" I asked her.

The next time I saw Spook Laurette was with me. It was night, during one of those heavy summer rainstorms that come up so suddenly. We were having dinner on the covered terrace of the local restaurant. Padding up the street came a dog, head down, tail down, looking as miserable as only an Irish setter can when it's soaking wet. As the dog came into the light cast by the terrace lamps, I said, "That looks like Spook." I must have pronounced the name quite loudly, for the dog stopped and his head came up. It was Spook.

He pushed in the screen door, walked across the flagged terrace, water dripping from his matted coat, and came up to my side. He stood there looking up into my face for a minute, then, without a bark or a wag of his tail, curled up on the stone at my feet. He dropped his head on his paws, but never once closed his eyes. He watched every move I made, just the way he used to. Four years, four long years, I thought, and I felt choked up. The waitress brought our food, and at the sight of the wet dog, she said, "Here, you—"

"Let him be!" I said, so sharply that the woman was startled. Laurette explained to her. Once during the meal I got up to go into the bar. Spook got up and went with me, all the way there and back, his head so close to my leg that my trousers brushed against him.

When we left the restaurant, Spook followed us. When I opened the door of the car, he was first in, over the front seat and into his accustomed place in the right-hand back corner, his head pressed against the window.

"What are you going to do?" Laurette asked me.

"What can I do on a night like this?" I asked.

She nodded her head understandingly. "Let's go home then," she said.

We took Spook back to the little house with us. The open fire dried out his coat, and the feathers on his legs and tail got all curly blond. He lay there on the floor be-

tween Laurette's chair and my desk, his head toward me.
If I stood up, he was instantly on his feet. At about ten
o'clock, exactly as he had always done, he came over to
my chair, placed a paw on my knee, cocked his head to
one side, and gazed silently up into my face.

"What does he want?" Laurette asked.

"Out," I said, and I got up and opened the screen door
for him. The rain had stopped and the moon had risen.
Staring out into the darkness that had swallowed up the
dog, I said over my shoulder, "Well, that's that, I guess.
He'll go home now to wherever home is." And for an
instant I was filled with regret that I had so sternly held
myself back from touching him or even so much as speaking to him in the old intimate way.

Back at the desk I couldn't work. I stared at the blank
paper in my typewriter. The paper didn't exist for me,
nor the room—not even Laurette existed for me. I was
caught in the world outside the house; my ears strained
for the slightest whisper or rustle in the grass.

At about eleven, two quick, imperious barks sounded
outside the screen door. Laurette lifted her eyebrows in-
quiringly. "He wants in," I told her. I jumped up from
my chair and stood there helplessly in the center of the
room, not knowing what to do.

"Well, go on," Laurette said. "Let him in. We'll talk
later."

So I let him in, and when he went to bed he took his
usual position on the floor beside my bed. I could hear
him there, breathing softly in the darkness.

Laurette talked to me. "This is why I didn't want you
to see him again," she said.

"But he was only two years old when I left him, and after four years who would believe he'd remember this way?" His act of remembrance had been with me all evening; it was a wonderful thing. "It's just as if I had never gone away," I said.

"Try not to think of that," Laurette said. "Think of Spook. Think how beautiful and fit he is, and remember that he's leading the proper life for a dog. A whole valley to roam in. What kind of a life would he lead with us in the city? With both of us working, what would he have? A walk on a lead twice a day? Never any grass or sun, never to run free. You wouldn't want to take him back to that now that he's had the other, would you?"

"But I'm not doing anything," I protested. "I haven't even petted him. He's doing it all himself."

"The decision is up to you. You have to make it."

"All right then," I said. "We'll take him back to the Crokers' tomorrow." She reached across and patted my arm and said no more. I don't know how long it took me to get to sleep that night. All I remember now is that once during the night I heard Spook get up and change position. I heard him hit the floor with a thud the way setters do. As he stretched out again I heard him sigh, a sound that seemed to contain all the contentment of the world.

We started for the Croker place at noon the next day. It was blazing hot. We drove the five miles in complete silence, except for Spook, who occasionally would whine anxiously deep in his throat.

We turned off the road and up the lane and circled the drive of the big house. When I took Spook out of the car, my fingers tight about his collar, he was whining continually, and nothing in the world could have made me look into his eyes.

The boy I had seen in the pasture that other morning answered my knock; he looked astounded at seeing me with the dog. And all the time I talked to him, explaining what had happened, Spook kept pulling to break my hold on his collar. At last the boy understood the situation and took hold of Spook's collar, and I got back in the car and drove off.

We had gone only about a mile on the macadam when I saw him in the rear-view mirror. He was racing after the car, running his heart out. "That fool kid let him loose!" I said, and put on speed, but I couldn't tear my eyes from the mirror. He kept running and running, and the sun kept beating down on him, and I knew he would never give up.

Suddenly Laurette said in a tense voice, "Do you want to kill him? Stop the car! Stop the car! Do you hear?"

Pulling off the road onto the grass, I got out of the car and waited. Spook came up and sank exhausted at my feet, his chest laboring painfully, his tongue hanging from his mouth. There was a little sound from the car, and I turned around. Laurette was crying softly, the tears running down her cheeks.

"Spook, poor Spook," she kept saying through her sobs. "Don't worry anymore, not anymore, please. We'll take him with us. It'll be all right, fine. You can walk him in the morning before you go to work, and I'll come home on my lunch hour and take him then. And Bessy won't mind taking him out once in the afternoon." Bessy was our maid. "We'll manage somehow," Laurette said.

I patted her shoulder and gave her my handkerchief. I put Spook in the back of the car and turned it around and headed back for the Croker place. Laurette put a restraining hand on my arm. "No, dear," I said, "it wouldn't work. Last night you talked with your head. Believe me, the head's better."

This time I told the boy to lock Spook in the house, and when we drove away I drove very fast and Laurette said nothing about the speed.

All this took place more than three years ago. Today I rarely think of Spook, consciously anyway. But three or four times every year I have a recurring dream, a horrible nightmare.

The scene of the dream is always the same: the stretch of macadam highway. I am myself in the car, and at the same time I am Spook, and I run and I run and the car never stops, and the hard, cruel road hits my paws and the sun beats down on me, and I keep saying over and over again, "He doesn't want me, he doesn't want me." And then I feel a grief so sharp that I cannot contain it, and my heart swells and swells and threatens to burst with the sheer pity of it. At this point I always wake up in a cold sweat and I slip quietly out of bed, for I have never told Laurette about the recurring dream.

I go into the living room and light a cigarette and stare out the window. The streets are empty; the dark, cold stone houses hem them in. There are no trees, and that helps. I force myself to remember Spook as I saw him that day in the green pasture running free, with the soft grass beneath his feet and the wind whipping his ears back and the sun striking from his gleaming copper coat. That helps, too.

I put out my cigarette and go back to bed and to sleep. But even now, three years later, even now after writing it all down, I do not know whether the decision I made for Spook was right or wrong.

The Emissary   *Ray Bradbury*

Martin knew it was autumn again, for Dog ran into the
house bringing wind and frost and a smell of apples turned
to cider under trees. In dark clock springs of hair, Dog
fetched goldenrod, dust of farewell summer, acorn husk,
hair of squirrel, feather of departed robin, sawdust from
fresh-cut cordwood, and leaves like charcoals shaken from
a blaze of maple trees. Dog jumped. Showers of brittle
fern, blackberry vine, marsh grass sprang over the bed
where Martin shouted. No doubt, no doubt of it at all, this
incredible beast was October!

"Here, boy, here!"

And Dog settled to warm Martin's body with all the bonfires and subtle burnings of the season, to fill the room with soft or heavy, wet or dry odors of far traveling. In spring, he smelled of lilac, iris, lawn-mowered grass; in summer, ice-cream-moustached, he came pungent with firecracker, Roman candle, pinwheel, baked by the sun. But autumn! Autumn!

"Dog, what's it like outside?"

And lying there, Dog told as he always told. Lying there, Martin found autumn as in the old days before sickness bleached him white on his bed. Here was his contact, his carryall, the quick-moving part of himself he sent with a yell to run and return, circle and scent, collect and deliver the time and texture of worlds in town, country, by creek, river, lake, down-cellar, up-attic, in closet or coal bin. Ten dozen times a day he was gifted with sunflower seed, cinder path, milkweed, horse chestnut, or full flame smell of pumpkin. Through the loomings of the universe Dog shuttled; the design was hid in his pelt. Put out your hand; it was there.

But he knew without hearing where Dog had rattled down hills, where autumn lay in cereal crispness, where children lay in funeral pyres, in rustling heaps, the leaf-buried but watchful dead, as Dog and the world blew by. Martin trembled his fingers, searched the thick fur, read the long journey. Through stubbled fields, over glitters of ravine creek, down marbled spread of cemetery yard, into woods. In the great season of spices and race incense, now Martin ran through his emissary around, about, and home!

The bedroom door opened. "That dog of yours is in trouble again."

Mother brought in a tray of fruit salad, cocoa, and toast, her blue eyes snapping.

"Mother . . . ."

"Always digging places. Dug a hole in Miss Tarkin's garden this morning. She's spittin' mad. That's the fourth hole he's dug there this week."

"Maybe he's looking for something."

"Fiddlesticks, he's too darned curious. If he doesn't behave he'll be locked up."

Martin looked at this woman as if she were a stranger. "Oh, you wouldn't do that! How would I learn anything? How would I find things out if Dog didn't tell me?"

Mom's voice was quieter. "Is that what he does—tell you things?"

"There's nothing I don't know when he goes out and around and back, *nothing* I can't find out from him!"

They both sat looking at Dog and the dry strewings of mold and seed over the quilt.

"Well, if he'll just stop digging where he shouldn't, he can run all he wants," said Mother.

"Here, boy, here!"

And Martin snapped a tin note to the dog's collar: *My Owner Is Martin Smith. Ten Years Old. Sick in Bed. Visitors Welcome.*

Dog barked. Mother opened the downstairs door and let him out.

Martin sat listening.

Far off and away he could hear Dog in the quiet autumn rain that was falling now. He could hear the barking-jingling fade, rise, fade again as he cut down alley, over lawn, to fetch back Mr. Holloway and the oiled metallic smell of the snowflake-interiored watches he repaired in his home shop. Or maybe he would bring Mr. Jacobs, the grocer, whose clothes were rich with lettuce, celery, tomatoes, and the secret-tinned and hidden smell of the red demons stamped on cans of deviled ham. Mr. Jacobs and his unseen pink-meat devils waved often from the yard below. Or Dog brought Mr. Jackson, Mrs. Gillespie, Mr. Smith, Mrs. Holmes, any friend or near friend, encountered, concerned, begged, worried, and at last shepherded home for lunch or tea and cookies.

Now, listening, Martin heard Dog below, with footsteps moving in a light rain behind him. The downstairs bell rang, Mom opened the door, light voices murmured. Martin sat forward, face shining. The stairsteps creaked. A young woman's voice laughed quietly. Miss Haight, of course, his teacher from school!

The bedroom door sprang open. Martin had company.

Morning, afternoon, evening, dawn and dusk, sun and moon circles with Dog, who faithfully reported temperatures of turf and air, color of earth and tree, consistency of mist or rain, but, most important of all, brought back again and again and again Miss Haight.

On Saturday, Sunday, and Monday she baked Martin orange-iced cupcakes, brought him library books about dinosaurs and cavemen. On Tuesday, Wednesday, and Thursday somehow he beat her at dominoes, somehow she lost at checkers, and soon, she cried, he'd defeat her handsomely at chess. On Friday, Saturday, and Sunday they talked and never stopped talking, and she was so young and laughing and handsome and her hair was a soft, shining brown like the season outside the window, and she walked clear, clean, and quick, a heartbeat warm in the bitter afternoon when he heard it. Above all, she had the secret of signs and could read and interpret Dog and the symbols she searched out and plucked forth from his coat with her miraculous fingers. Eyes shut, softly laughing, in a Gypsy's voice, she divined the world from the treasures in her hands.

And on Monday afternoon, Miss Haight was dead.

Martin sat up in bed, slowly. "Dead?" he whispered.

Dead, said his mother, yes, dead, killed in a car accident a mile out of town. Dead, yes, dead, which meant cold to Martin, which meant silence and whiteness and winter come long before its time. Dead, silent, cold, white. The thoughts circled around, blew down, and settled in whispers.

Martin held Dog, thinking, turned to the wall. The lady with the autumn-colored hair. The lady with the laughter that was very gentle and never made fun, and the eyes that watched your mouth to see everything you ever said. The other-half-of-autumn lady, who told what was left untold by Dog, about the world. The heartbeat at the still center of gray afternoon. The heartbeat fading. . . .

"Mom? What do they do in the graveyard, Mom, under the ground? Just lay there?"

"*Lie* there."

"Lie there? Is that all they do? It doesn't sound like much fun."

"For goodness' sake, it's not made out to be fun."

"Why don't they jump up and run around once in a while if they get tired lying there? God's pretty silly—"

"Martin!"

"Well, you'd think He'd treat people better than to tell them to lie still for keeps. That's impossible. Nobody can do it. I tried once. Dog tries. I tell him, 'dead Dog!' He plays dead awhile, then gets sick and tired and wags his tail or opens one eye and looks at me, bored. Boy, I bet sometimes those graveyard people do the same, huh, Dog?"

Dog barked.

"Be still with that kind of talk!" said Mother.

Martin looked off into space. "Bet that's exactly what they do," he said.

Autumn burned the trees bare and ran Dog still farther around, fording creek, prowling graveyard as was his custom, and back in the dusk to fire off volleys of barking that shook windows wherever he turned.

In the late, last days of October, Dog began to act as if the wind had changed and blew from a strange country. He stood quivering on the porch below. He whined, his eyes fixed at the empty land beyond town. He brought no visitors for Martin. He stood for hours each day, as if leashed, trembling, then shot away straight, as if someone had called. Each night he returned later, with no one following. Each night Martin sank deeper and deeper in his pillow.

"Well, people are busy," said Mother. "They haven't time to notice the tag Dog carries. Or they mean to come to visit, but forget."

But there was more to it than that. There was the fevered shining in Dog's eyes, and his whimpering tic late at night in some private dream. His shivering in the dark, under the bed. The way he sometimes stood half the night, looking at Martin as if some great and impossible secret was his and he knew no way to tell it save by savagely thumping his tail or turning in endless circles, never to lie down, spinning and spinning again.

On October 30, Dog ran out and didn't come back at

all, even when after supper Martin heard his parents call
and call. The hour grew late, the streets and pavements
stood empty, the air moved cold about the house, and
there was nothing, nothing.

Long after midnight, Martin lay watching the world
beyond the cool, clear glass windows. Now there was not
even autumn, for there was no Dog to fetch it in. There
would be no winter, for who could bring the snow to melt
in his hands? Father, Mother? No, not the same. They
couldn't play the game with its special secrets and rules,
its sounds and pantomines. No more seasons. No more
time. The go-between, the emissary, was lost to the wild
throngings of civilization, poisoned, stolen, hit by a car,
left somewhere in a culvert. . . .

Sobbing, Martin turned his face to his pillow. The world
was a picture under glass, untouchable. The world was
dead.

Martin twisted in bed, and in three days the last Halloween pumpkins were rotting in trash cans, papier-
mâché skulls and witches were burned on bonfires, and
ghosts were stacked on shelves with other linens until next
year.

To Martin, Halloween had been nothing more than
one evening when tin horns cried off in the cold autumn
stars, children blew like goblin leaves along the flinty
walks, flinging their heads, or cabbages, soap-writing names
or similar magic symbols on icy windows. All of it as
distant, unfathomable, and nightmarish as a puppet show
seen from so many miles away that there is no sound or
meaning.

For three days in November, Martin watched alternate
light and shadow sift across his ceiling. The fire pageant

was over forever; autumn lay in cold ashes. Martin sank deeper, yet deeper, in white marble layers of bed, motionless, listening, always listening.

Friday evening his parents kissed him good-night and walked out of the house into the hushed cathedral weather toward a motion-picture show. Miss Tarkins from next door stayed on in the parlor below until Martin called down he was sleepy, then took her knitting off home.

In silence, Martin lay following the great move of stars down a clear and moonlit sky, remembering nights such as this when he'd spanned the town with Dog ahead, behind, around about, tracking the green-plush ravine, lapping slumbrous streams gone milky with the fullness of the moon, leaping cemetery tombstones while whispering the marble names. On, quickly on, through shaved meadows where the only motion was the off-on quivering of stars, to streets where shadows would not stand aside for you but crowded all the pavements for mile on mile. Run now, run! Chasing, being chased by bitter smoke, fog, mist wind, ghost of mind, fright of memory. Home, safe, sound, snug warm, asleep. . . .

Nine o'clock. Chime. The drowsy clock in the deep stairwell below. Chime. Dog, come home and run the world with you. Dog, bring a thistle with frost on it, or bring nothing else but the wind. Dog, where are you? Oh, listen now. I'll call.

Martin held his breath. Way off somewhere—a sound.

Martin rose up, trembling. There again—the sound.

So small a sound, like a sharp needlepoint brushing the sky long miles and many miles away. The dreamy echo of a dog barking.

The sound of a dog crossing fields and farms, dirt roads

and rabbit paths, running, running, letting out great barks of steam, cracking the night. The sound of a circling dog that came and went, lifted and faded, opened up, shut in, moved forward, went back, as if the animal were kept by someone on a fantastically long chain. As if the dog were running and someone whistled under the chestnut trees, in mold shadow, tar shadow, moon shadow, walking, and the dog circled back and sprang out again toward home.

Dog! Martin thought. Oh, Dog, come home, boy! Listen, oh, listen, where you been? Come on, boy, make tracks!

Five, ten, fifteen minutes; near, very near, the bark, the sound. Martin cried out, thrust his feet from the bed, leaned to the window. Dog! Listen, boy! Dog! Dog! He said it over and over. Dog! Dog! Wicked Dog, run off and gone all these days Bad Dog, good Dog. Home, boy, hurry, and bring what you can!

Near now, near, up the street, barking to knock clapboard housefronts with sound, whirl iron cocks on rooftops in the moon, firing off volleys. Dog! Now at the door below. . . .

Martin shivered. Should he run, let Dog in, or wait for Mom and Dad? Wait? Oh, God, wait? But what if Dog ran off again? No, he'd go down, snatch the door wide, yell, grab Dog in, and run upstairs so fast, laughing, crying, holding tight, that—

Dog stopped barking.

Hey! Martin almost broke the window, jerking to it.

Silence, as if someone had told Dog to hush now, hush, hush.

A full minute passed. Martin clenched his fists.

Below, a faint whimpering.

Then slowly the downstairs front door opened. Someone was kind enough to have opened the door for Dog. Of course! Dog had brought Mr. Jacobs or Mr. Gillespie or Miss Tarkins, or—

The downstairs door shut.

Dog raced upstairs, whining, flung himself on the bed.

"Dog, Dog, where've you *been*? What've you *done*! Dog, Dog!" And he crushed Dog hard and long to himself, weeping. Dog, Dog. He laughed and shouted. Dog! But after a moment he stopped laughing and crying.

He pulled back away. He held the animal and looked at him, eyes widening.

The odor coming from Dog was different. It was a smell of strange earth. It was a smell of night within night, the smell of digging down deep in shadow through earth that had lain cheek by jowl with things that were long hidden and decayed. A stinking and rancid soil fell away in clods of dissolution from Dog's muzzle and paws. He had dug deep. He had dug very deep indeed. That was it, wasn't it? Wasn't it? *Wasn't* it!

What kind of message was this from Dog? What could such a message mean? The stench, the ripe and awful cemetery earth.

Dog was a bad dog, digging where he shouldn't. Dog was a good dog, always making friends. Dog loved people. Dog brought them home.

And now, moving up the dark hall stairs at intervals, came the sound of feet. One foot dragged after the other, painfully, slowly, slowly, slowly.

Dog shivered. A rain of strange night earth fell seething on the bed.

Dog turned. The bedroom door whispered in.

Martin had company.

Choice
of the Litter
Roderick Lull

It was to him a very simple thing, and the wonder was
that the others, the older ones, were so stupid and confused. It was only a matter of going back a few years to
when he was ten, her age, and thinking as he had thought
then. The old urges and desires and faiths came back,
and along with them the memory of the path, half forgotten now, that followed down the tiny stream through
the woods and came at the end to the cave. It was there,
he decided firmly, that the lost girl had gone.

He stood a little distance from the group of men, watching the captain, noting his taut face and nervous hands.

He had always thought of the captain and of the captain's daughter as beings apart—as somehow Olympian people with whom he and his kind had little or nothing in common. He had felt that way for years, ever since the time his uncle had left him the fifty dollars and he had gone, nervous and hesitating, to his father and said that he meant to spend it for one of the captain's fine springer spaniels.

He could remember still his father's dark, bloodshot eyes looking at him with infinite weariness, and he could still hear his father's voice saying, "So you're getting big ideas. Well, you'll get over them before you're much older. Them fancy dogs is for people like the captain. Not for our kind. Keep that in your mind, if you got one. We ain't like the captain. We only work a piece of his land."

The money had been spent for clothes for the family and a much-needed new stove, and the little that was left had gone into the meager budget.

So it was a strange thing to see the captain now as only a worried and indecisive man, a man like other men, gesturing and shaking his head and saying over and over, "We've got to find her before another night comes. You sure you asked at every house along the Toll Road, Tom? I'm not satisfied with the way we combed that hill country, Jim." He looked at them with bright, agonized eyes.

Ben Frazier went down the road then, tightening the loose knot in the rope that served him for a belt. The captain sure set a mighty store by his daughter, he thought.

He pulled the old straw hat down against the sun and walked faster. Soon he turned off on the little abandoned logging road and, a hundred yards along, left that to fight his way through brush to the forgotten trail. He saw a strip of bark torn from a log, broken branches, and a shoe print in the mud by a small spring. He smiled. He had been right; he knew where the lost girl was.

He found her at the old cave as he had expected, and she was too tired and frightened to answer when he told her shortly that they were going home. They walked side by side up to the house.

He was about to leave her when he heard a call and saw the captain coming toward them. He shifted uncomfortably from one foot to the other while the captain bent and held his daughter close. Then the captain, clinging to the girl's small, limp hand, rose and turned to him, the tightness gone from his face now, the lines fewer and not so deep. He said, "I've seen you around. You're Frazier's son, aren't you?"

"Yes, sir."

The captain ran a hand through his hair. "What do you want, boy? You've got something coming."

He shook his head and turned away. "That's all right."

The captain laughed. "Maybe she would have come home by herself today. But saving me an hour or two of the worry is worth plenty. Tell me what you'd like, boy."

He drew a sharp breath. He thought of the kennel back of the house and of the fine new litter. The captain was a dog man. He raised the best springers in the state. The captain owned the greatest springer that had ever lived, and this dog had sired the new litter. But dogs like that were rich men's dogs.

He settled his feet in the roadbed. "I'd like a dog. One of your dogs. Only I know it's too much to be asking."

The captain looked at him for a moment, then nodded and said, "Nothing's been sold out of the new litter. You can have your choice of it. I didn't plan to sell for two weeks. If you want to wait, you'll be able to make a better pick. I'm promising you I'll sell nothing until you've had your pick."

He had to think the words over in his mind before they had any meaning. Then he had to look into the captain's face again to make sure he wasn't having the cruelest kind of sport that any man had ever had. And when the words came out of his throat at last, they came in a voice he had never heard before. "If you mean it, if it's all right, I'll pick now."

It was a litter of eight. He knelt and ran his hands over them lovingly. He looked at their tremendous feet and their bright, sad faces; he watched the eternal movement of their sterns and thought that surely he was dreaming. After a long time he stood up and saw that the captain, whom he had forgotten, was still leaning against the fence.

The captain smiled at him. "If you want my advice, I'd take that big fellow. I never saw a better chest, and if he turns gun-shy, I'll eat him."

The captain's advice was honest. Ben had watched dogs all his knowing life, and this was the likeliest specimen. Most men would take him. Only there was another of the males that he had been watching. A little small maybe, and he certainly didn't stand out in a litter fine as this. He couldn't have told why he preferred him to the rest. It was something felt, something beyond and alien to words. "I'd like him," he said.

The captain looked puzzled. "He seems to me a little on the nervous side. But it's your choice, not mine, and I've made my mistakes."

"I'll take him along now, if it suits you."

The captain nodded, and he picked the dog up. He heard the captain telling him to come back in the morning, and they'd make a deal about food. He wouldn't have a dog fed wrong, and feeding right was an expensive business for a man who didn't own a kennel.

Ben said, "Thank you, sir," and started home. A little wind had come up, and he put the dog gently inside his shirt against his skin, and very soon its frightened trembling stopped.

He did not go directly home. He knew with grim certainty what would be said when he arrived there carrying the dog.

He went into a field where the clover was deep and soft as an animal's pelt and put the dog down. The dog looked up at him, pricking his ears, his muzzle quivering and eager. Even in his great-footed awkwardness was a grace, a fineness of movement that was surer proof of his breeding than the writing on his pedigree. The dog came to him when he called, and he stroked him for a few moments, then stood up, suddenly austere. You could harm the finest dog ever born with an excess of attention.

He went home then, and when he met his father he spoke first. "This is my dog," he said softly. "The captain's girl got lost. I found her. He gave me the dog."

His father looked at the dog with fathomless eyes. "So the captain did. I guess you're one of the captain's buddies. No doubt you'll be going into the city soon to buy yourself some of those swell clothes like he wears. A blooded dog like that expects a lot of a man, all right. Why, he wouldn't lower himself to bark at anyone like me."

Ben said nothing. The dog lay at his feet on his back, the four immense paws waving. And while he looked at

him he changed from a puppy into a grown dog, all grace
and power and sureness and intelligence, the finest sight
any man's eyes had ever seen. It was as if the dog's whole
great career had been graphed out, right down to his final
victories in the great National trials that rich men spent
thousands trying to win and failed a hundred times for
each time they succeeded. He started to turn away.

"You take that dog back."

"I'm not taking him back." He said the words without
passion, the way you say a fact beyond denial.

When his father turned suddenly on his heel and went
into the house, he knew he had won the first round. He
took the dog to the barn, where there was old wire and
boards, and started the job of building an enclosure and
a doghouse.

It seemed to him that each day really began at evening,
when he was done with his work and could have some
time for the spaniel. He was prepared for his father's giving him more and more jobs to do. He made no complaint.
He worked harder than ever in his life and knew no weariness. The most onerous work was easy when you knew
that once it was finished you could do what was closest to
your heart. He and his father talked little. His mother
had nothing to say concerning the dog; it was obvious that
she thought of him as only a creature that ate food and
barked at nothing and tried to come into the house where
he wasn't wanted.

He thought a great deal about a name for the dog. You
couldn't call one of the captain's spaniels Bill or Pete or
Boy. He had to have a dignified name with style. It came
to him in the middle of one night. The nearest town was

Derrydale, and the captain had given him the dog. Derry-dale Captain. Derry for short.

He worked slowly, patiently, first teaching the dog obedience. He taught Derry to come to him, to walk at heel, and to sit at his feet without jumping on him. After each lesson he lay on the ground and let the dog run about as he pleased, watching him all the time.

Often he talked to Derry, telling him in short, definite words what his life was to be. He held him by the scruff of his neck and tried to make him understand all that was wanted of him, all that he must do. Once his father came up to him at such a time and announced his arrival by a laugh. "That must be a wonderful dog you got. Talks English just like a human, I see. Or maybe you're a little cracked in the head."

He stood up and faced his father, feeling an impotence, a harsh knowledge of his inability to say in words the thoughts that boiled within him. When he turned away without answering, his father laughed again, a long laugh. He wondered, his blood pulsing hotly, that any man could be so unfeeling. Then his father walked away almost jauntily, as if he had achieved a victory. He had no heart for more training that evening and put Derry into his kennel. He awoke in the middle of the night feeling deep shame that he had let himself be so disturbed by nothing. His father was only a man who did not see as he did.

Twice each week he went to the big house to get food for Derry. He didn't feel that this was charity; he and the captain knew that such a dog must have certain foods and that was all there was to it. Sometimes one of the hands would get the food for him. Other times the captain would be there, and they would talk.

"How's he coming along? Taught him anything yet?"

"He's coming pretty good."

"Bring him up next time you come. I'd like to see him."

"Yes, sir," he always said. But he didn't bring the dog next time. He didn't intend to. He didn't want the captain or anyone else to see Derry until he was right.

One night Derry looked poorly. His eyes were watery, the underlids half closed. He felt a surge of fear like a knife between his ribs, and he stayed up all night keeping the dog warm, watching and waiting, feeding him warm milk. In the morning Derry was definitely improved. It wasn't distemper, after all, just a slight cold.

His father was waiting for him. "Did you go to bed last night?"

"No."

"You stayed up with that dog. I suppose he coughed or something. Well, I'm telling you this, I'm not letting any dog interfere with the work around here. I've let you keep him so long as you held your end up. This is too much. No man's fit to work without sleeping. And—"

He said, "You'll have a better idea when the day's over what I can do."

He drove himself to the most productive day's work of his life. When his eyes were burning and half blind for lack of sleep and his muscles fairly screamed for rest, he increased his exertions. His father said nothing.

The next morning Derry was in perfect fettle, jumping at the wire and crying to get out for a run. He allowed himself to pet him a little longer than usual that morning.

Derry took to retrieving quickly, but he had a naturally hard mouth, and many hours of work with a feather-covered ball in which needles were cunningly placed were needed to break him. When Derry was six months old, it was late summer and time for him to know the sight and sound and scent of pheasant.

Ben took him into the remote corn patch one Sunday morning. He fastened a long line to the round collar of saddle leather that he had bought with money long saved for another purpose. Then they started slowly through the corn, Ben speaking softly to Derry now and then to restrain his bouncing eagerness. A young hen flushed five feet ahead and rose cackling into the air. Derry broke and Ben called to him, not raising his voice. The dog rushed on, barking now, oblivious of everything but the bird soaring toward the shelter of the woods. Ben held the line firm, and Derry tumbled over backward, gave a small cry, more of surprise than pain, and came trembling to his feet.

Ben went on as if nothing had happened. The same thing happened half a dozen times. After that Derry stopped dead in his tracks when his name was spoken, even when three birds were flushed at once not ten feet from him.

They went home at noon, and Ben himself was trembling with excitement. His father was sitting smoking in a rickety chair in the sunshine, and Ben was so eager to talk to someone that he blurted out the news as soon as he reached him. "You should have seen him with the checkline. He got onto it in no time. I know it took weeks to break some of the captain's good dogs. I tell you this dog's got something no other dog I ever saw has."

His father blew a spiral of gray smoke into the clear air. "Wonderful," he said. "Maybe he can smell out a gold mine. I hate to remind you of it, but we're poor people and we're supposed to work at things that make a little money."

"A good bird dog's worth money," he said. "Big money."

"That may be," his father said. "I don't doubt it. Now if you think your high-toned dog's worth something—"

"There's not enough money in the world to buy this dog."

His father made no answer. Ben walked quickly away. He had been burdened suddenly with a dark fear that clung to him stubbornly, try as he might to shake it off.

He felt his heart beating hard and too fast the day he first went into the field with his old hammer gun and a pocket full of shells he had loaded himself with light charges. He let Derry go a long way off, then fired. Derry started, looked about, and cowered, belly to the ground. Ben walked toward him, firing twice as he came; the dog broke and ran out of sight into the woods. He called him, but Derry was a long time coming back.

When the dog returned to him, shaking as if with fever, he stroked him lightly until the fear had passed. Then they returned home.

For five days he put the tin plate of food down each evening at feeding time and waited until Derry came for it. Then he fired into the air. The dog ran into his kennel, and Ben took away the plate. On the fifth day the dog's flanks, to Ben's agonized eyes, were thin as paper. He wanted to give in, to let Derry eat in peace, and afterward to sit by him and let him lick his hands and look up at him worshipfully with his great spaniel eyes. But he steeled himself and waited.

The sixth day Derry ate, though he trembled still. Ben praised him extravagantly, and after that there was no trouble.

He worked until darkness made work impossible the

week before the opening of the pheasant season. He walked the five miles into town and back one Sunday to buy his license, then stayed up late that night to load shells and clean the old shotgun. The evening before he told his father he wanted the day off.

"I been working extra," he explained quietly. "I've done a good day's work ahead and more."

"And if I said no—"

"I'd go anyway. I have to go. This is my first chance to see what he can do. Only . . . I'd rather have your say-so."

His father shrugged. "Do what you like. If you're as crazy—dog crazy—as that, there's nothing I can do to help it."

He chose a place where no others were apt to go. He was there before dawn broke, waiting with Derry pressed against his knees. He didn't expect many birds. It was not a good place. If he could only bring one or two down he'd be satisfied. Then he'd know where Derry stood.

They worked two hours, the dog crossing and quartering the ground, before a bird was raised. It was a fine shot, going away, and he made a clean kill. He saw the cock fall, and the dog go forward to it. He stood still, his hands shaking so he could hardly support the gun. Then, through misty eyes, he saw Derry coming to him, the pheasant in his jaws. He straightened and waited. The dog sat down before him and placed the bird lightly in his hand.

He drew a long breath. He'd seen the captain's dogs work, and only one of them handled a bird in handsomer fashion. That dog was the champion who had sired Derry.

He said aloud, "You know, you, there's no dog young

as you in the world that's in your class. And someday there won't be any dog in the world as good as you, no matter how old and smart he is."

He got his last bird just before it became too dark to see. Derry raised it out of a small corn patch, and Ben swung and brought it down with a side-angle shot. A moment later Derry retrieved. It was then that he felt someone watching him.

He turned and fifty feet away saw a dark figure. The captain's voice came floating across to him, soft-syllabled and obviously excited.

"That was good," he said. "That was fine. I enjoyed seeing that."

"I didn't know you were here, sir."

"Heard shooting and thought I'd wander down and see who it was. Truth is, I'd an idea it might be you." The captain approached and stooped to touch and examine Derry. "And I would never have picked this one," he said. "I always pride myself for picking 'em young and picking 'em right, too. I congratulate you."

"I guess I was lucky."

"Maybe. But there wasn't any luck about the way you trained your dog. You did train him yourself?"

"Yes, sir."

"Have any help at all?"

"No, sir. My father don't care about dogs." He was sorry at once for saying that; to tell a man like the captain that another man didn't care for dogs was to brand him an outcast.

"I see. What's the dog's name?"

Ben felt his face redden as he told him. But the captain laughed and clapped him on the back and said that was a mighty fine compliment. He'd never had a finer one, the captain said, and he was grateful and happy for it. Then he said, and there was a serious note to his voice, "I'd like you to stop in at the house a minute. There's something I want to talk to you about."

Ben said, "Yes, sir." As they walked along in silence he felt a sharp, quick sense of foreboding that robbed him of all the pleasure of the day. But he told himself it was ridiculous; the captain was his friend. . . .

The captain led him to a small study. "Ben," he said, "I'm looking for a good young dog—a real field-trial dog, a dog that has a chance to win the National. That dog of yours, that Derry, might be what I'm looking for. I've a hunch he is."

Ben looked at the captain, then away. He felt real fear now, cold and hard, and wished desperately that he hadn't come. He drew a breath that hurt and said, "Yes, sir."

"Now I don't want you to think of how you got your dog at all. Don't think you owe me any favors. You don't, and that's a fact. He's your dog, just as much as if you'd come to my kennel and paid a big price for him. But I'm going to make you a proposition. I'm going to offer you five hundred dollars for that dog. And on top of it, the choice of any other pup I've got. You're perfectly free to take it or leave it."

Five hundred dollars meant riches such as Ben had never known. It meant lifting the ceiling of fear that pressed his family down. But Derry. He could not let himself think of Derry. It seemed now as if this had been predestined from the beginning. If he had only been wiser, he could have seen it coming, sure and certain as the procession of the days. He could, of course, refuse. For a moment he clutched at the thought as if it were a sturdy floating plank and he a boy drowning. But no matter what, you always knew what you had to do. There was something that made you do it out of respect for your own self.

He said, "Yes, sir, Captain."

"It's a deal," the captain said. He opened a desk drawer, found a checkbook, and wrote a check. He handed it to Ben. "Now we'll go out to the kennel, and you can have your pick again. And, boy, I'll bet you pick right."

Ben stood up. He said quietly, "Thank you, sir, but I don't want another dog. I'll be going now."

"Then you're entitled to a hundred more."

He didn't answer that. He turned and hurried away. He heard the captain's voice with a worried note to it, "Well, then I'll send it down to you."

Outside he did not look at Derry. He told him roughly to stay where he was and did not look back as the captain led him away.

At home he put the check on the table and told his father what had happened. His father picked up the check and examined it, holding it as delicately as if it were some fragile bit of china. Then he laid it down.

Ben said, "It's yours. To do with what you want."

His father shook his head. He looked past the boy above his head, as if there were something of great interest on the wall opposite. "Thanks for your favors. I don't want no part of them. I got along and I always will. Maybe you'll want to be buying a car with it, like your rich friends have."

Ben stared at his father for a long time. His father's eyes never lowered. A sudden gust of wind came through the open window and blew the check to the floor. His father picked it up and put it in the drawer of the table. "It'll stay there, for all of me and your mother," he said. "You'll know where it is when you want it."

The days went by leadenly. At first it seemed that not having Derry was more than he could bear. Then one day he tore down the enclosure he had made and chopped the kennel into kindling. After that it was not so hard; it was as if with ax and hammer he had destroyed something that never should have been and so, in a strange sense, set himself free from a harsh bondage.

Half a dozen times he met the captain. Always he escaped as soon as he decently could, not asking about Derry. The captain mentioned the dog once. That was soon after the sale, and the captain asked if he'd like to come up for a hunt. He made some palpably false excuse, and the captain, nodding his head, said gently, "As you like, Ben. I know. But he's doing what he was made to do, and that's what any being should." The captain did not speak to him of Derry again.

He worked a day for a neighbor and earned enough cash to subscribe to a magazine devoted to field trials. The check still lay in the table drawer untouched, and with it the check for the additional hundred, which the captain had sent down by a servant. He read the magazine with infinite care, line by line, analyzing the dogs pictured and finding none that had the grace and power and perfection of Derry.

The first time he saw Derry's name the print seemed to leap from the page. It was in an article covering a tri-county trial, and it simply said that Derrydale Captain, owned by Captain Richard Harmon and handled by Joe

Bleecher, had placed second. Derry, the article went on, "ranged nicely and obviously had an excellent nose, but was not too well controlled."

He felt anger at the criticism, then wonder that Derry had come in second. Yet Bleecher was a famous trainer and handler to whom the captain sent many of his most promising dogs. It was ridiculous to think that the outcome would have been different had he been the handler that day, but that night he slept badly and dreamed of hunting with Derry, the dog that was the great champion of all the great champions of the world.

Derry's name appeared frequently after that: a third here, another second there, a first in one or two county trials where the competition was entirely unworthy of him. In the Western he did not place at all. Once there was a picture, a small one-column cut taken at a bad angle. He stood for minutes looking at it, miserable with the pictorial injustice of it.

He kept the magazines from his father's sight. He was always first at the mailbox around the period when they were due to arrive. Once his father caught him as he was reading one in the barn. His father's shadow fell across the page, and he looked up.

His father's eyes were wide and bright. "So our gentleman is improving his mind," he said. "It must be fine to be born to the purple."

Ben stood up, holding the words back that wanted to gush out. He rolled the magazine and stuffed it in a pocket. "I'm doing my work," he said.

His father smiled. "When you getting that car? The money's still in the drawer."

"It'll be there forever, far as I'm concerned."

"And me too. I guess the captain's ahead a nice piece of change. Well, if you can spare a minute, I can use you. If you can lower yourself to help."

The State Field Trial was coming up, and he read in his magazine that the captain had three dogs entered. Derry was one. Ben was hoeing the kitchen garden a day or two later when the captain's car came down the road and stopped near him. They shook hands gravely, and the captain stuffed tobacco into his pipe. "Ben, Derry's not going the way I hoped. I don't know whether you know."

"I know. I been reading about it."

"I figured him for maybe a National champion one day, and he couldn't win even those little trials. It's hard to blame Bleecher. He's got a record back of him."

Ben put the hoe down. "Bleecher ought to know as much as anybody."

"There's such a thing as a dog working right for only one man," the captain said. "It doesn't happen often, but it does happen."

He saw what was coming and wanted desperately to dodge it. He never wanted to see Derry again. That was one thing of which he was dead sure. And all he could do was to stand cowardlike before the captain and wait for for him to say what he knew he was going to say.

The captain put his pipe in his jacket pocket. "I want you to handle Derry in the State. I'll pay you the same as I would Bleecher—"

Ben broke in angrily. "I wouldn't take pay for a thing like that."

The captain eyed him curiously. "Well, we can argue that later. It's a detail. The point is, Will you do it?"

He looked away from the captain, seeking hastily for excuses. There was but one he could hit on that was at all valid. "We're busy now. I got to help. You know how it is this season."

"I know," the captain said. "I can send a man down to take your place."

"And my father— Well, he wouldn't like it. He doesn't think much of things like dog trials. For me, that is. And so I guess I'd better—"

"I can fix that with your father."

The way the captain said that sounded as if he thought his father nothing more than the servants that waited on table or the milch cows in the fine pastures. Ben stiffened and looked away stonily, his whole being an intense discomfort.

The captain watched him for a moment, then said, a different tone to his voice, "I'd think he'd be mighty proud of you handling a dog, maybe a winning dog, in that trial. After all, it's second only to the National. Yes, I've a feeling you'll be out there with Derry."

He could find nothing to say. The captain left him then, striding away to his car, and Ben watched him drive off.

When he looked toward the barn, he thought suddenly, his heart beating painfully hard, that he could see the wire enclosure and the doghouse within. He had to run his hand across his eyes to banish the strange illusion.

The captain came for him early, and they drove off into the cold, clear morning. His father had said good-by to him calmly, without comment, as if he were going off on some ordinary errand.

The captain drove fast, humming a tune, keeping his

short briar going like a furnace. Ben sat huddled in his ancient overcoat, his body a bundle of active nerves.

The trial was held at one of the great farms, twenty miles away, and long before they reached it the traffic grew thick. There were little cars and big cars, old cars and new, and the men who drove and rode in them were the big, smiling kind of men whose lives were given largely to their interest in sporting dogs.

They arrived and the captain got out, stretched, and pointed to a dog trailer hitched to a big coupe parked under a clump of trees. "That's Bleecher's rig," he said, without emphasis. "Derry's there."

Ben walked toward the trailer slowly, wondering if the dog would recognize him, hoping in one breath that he wouldn't and in the next knowing that it would be the cruelest blow he had ever suffered. Then Bleecher's boy, at the captain's nod, was opening the trailer back and Ben was saying, "Hello there, Derry," and the dog was hurling himself upon him. The dog barked twice, a high-pitched, staccato sound, and his eyes were blazing with eagerness. "Charge, Derry," and the dog hesitated, then dropped. He could resist no longer. He knelt and ran his hands lovingly down the smooth flanks, his head close to the dog's ears so that he could talk to him without being overheard.

Afterward he took him away into an empty field and gave him orders. He had him cross and quarter the ground and threw a rubber ball for him to retrieve. He was still busy with this when the captain appeared.

"You're going out in twenty minutes," the captain said. "How's he doing?"

"He's fine," Ben said. "He can win this."

"He's got tough competition. It's the best lot the State

ever saw, to my mind. There's a bitch here, shipped West by plane with her handler. She's been taking everything."

"He can win," Ben said again. The feel of the captain's hand on his shoulder was warm and pleasantly intimate, and he was glad that the captain said nothing more.

Afterward he tried to remember the day in full detail, and he failed. He remembered the beginning of it, when his own clothes seemed horribly shabby beside the fine boots and breeches and jackets of the big handlers. Then he put this firmly out of mind and concentrated on Derry. He never looked at another dog, and he never allowed himself to think that another dog might be going better. When he came to the trailer in the early afternoon, the captain spoke to him for the first time since the start. "Well done," the captain said.

He really saw the Eastern bitch for the first time when it was announced that she and Derry were to go out together; the judges had not been able to decide between them for first honors. She was a liver-and-white dog, delicately but beautifully made, with the fine eyes and full muzzle of a great line. He saw her handler looking at him, smiling curiously. He drew his shoulders back and made a little speech of resolution to himself. Then the guns were ready, and the judges were down the field in a little knot.

They were to have three birds each, and before Derry found his first a shot to the left meant the bitch had scored. Then Derry found two in quick order, and they were brought down and perfectly retrieved. The bitch found her second a moment later. Both found their third birds almost together; the shots came hardly a second apart.

It was over. As Ben walked back, Derry at heel, the sweat was dripping down his back and chest, though the

day was not warm. The captain had his arm and was saying, "I don't care which wins. I'll never forget this. You
even had Bleecher amazed. By the way, your father's over
there. He arrived a couple of hours ago."

Ben turned quickly and saw his father standing alone,
dressed in his ancient Sunday best, the dust thick on his
heavy, carefully polished shoes. There was about him an
immense pride, as if it were his protection against a world
full of humiliating and inimical things. He stood very
straight, and he looked like a man who was alone because
it was the way he wished to be, not because he had no one
to whom to turn for companionship.

Ben walked quickly toward him, thinking of how his
father must have come because he could not bring himself
to ask for a ride with Ben and the captain. The five-mile
walk to town, the search for a lift to reach the farm . . . .
Ben felt a strange, soft emotion that was entirely new to
him. He said, "Hello."

His father said, "Hello. I guess you did all right out
there."

Now he could almost feel the pride, as if it were a stone
wall between them. He said, "Listen . . . I want to tell
you . . . I want to tell you I'm mighty glad you came.
That makes it a good day. Sort of caps it off, as they say."

It seemed to Ben that a little of the ramrod stiffness went
out of his father's posture. "You mean that, Ben? You mean
that, like you said it?"

"Of course, I mean it."

His father smiled then, a wide, free smile that was reflected in his eyes. "I'm glad I came too. I guess there's a
lot more to these dog things than I knew."

The loudspeaker rumbled then, and a metallic voice

roared out. "The judges wish it announced that this was one of the closest and most brilliant contests in their experience. The winners are: first, Derrydale Captain, owned by Captain Richard Harmon, and handled today by Ben Frazier. Second—"

He heard no more, for there was a pounding as of surf in his ears, and his father and the captain were slapping him on the back and shouting. His mind was a spinning wheel of many colors that he thought would never stop.

It seemed a long time later that the captain was saying, "I've something to tell you. I'll make it short. It takes you to handle Derry. He's your dog. I'm giving him back to you, no strings attached. He won't work right for Bleecher or me or anyone else. I'm doing this because I want to, Ben."

The world was a calm and silent place now, and he looked up at the captain, knowing at once what his answer had to be, as if it had been all prepared by some portion of his mind that had the gift of anticipation. "I can't do that, sir."

The captain didn't answer, but waited.

"Because of Derry. He—he's got to do what he's supposed to do. Win the National. He can do it. It wouldn't be right not to give him the chance to do that."

"You mean," the captain said slowly, "there's a sort of absolute justice involved?"

"I guess that's it. I can help Mr. Bleecher so Derry will work for him. Derry'll do what I want. And I want him to be champion."

"I see." The captain looked away, and when he looked back his eyes were soft and moist as a spaniel's. "Only . . . the way you feel about Derry . . . I thought—"

"It's something I've got to work up to. To earn, I guess you'd say. And I will. I don't care how long it takes. I'm going to work and save for it."

The captain looked at him for a long time, then ran a big hand across his face. "Well. Well. Anyway, you go get your father. We're having a victory dinner tonight at the house. And I'm going to see to it your mother comes up too."

He found his father, and they went along to the car. His father walked slowly, his head down. Ben took hold of his arm. "I had an idea," he said. "About you and me and what to do with that money the captain paid for Derry. Maybe we could use it to start a little place of our own. We could work it on the side to begin with. I could help with all the work and then maybe get a pup cheap from the captain and start raising dogs and— Well, I thought something like that might be all right."

His father's shoulders bent forward a little, and he did not lift his head. "That was no thought of mine," he said slowly. Then words came out with a sudden burst, as if a dam had broken. "You could use that money for schooling. You ought to have more than just eighth grade. You could go to high school in town. The money would buy clothes and books, and I could make out here without you maybe, if I worked Sundays and a little extra evenings. I never wanted . . . I never wanted you should grow up ignorant like me."

Ben stopped short and faced his father with blazing eyes. "What a thing to say!" For the first time in his life he felt grown up, felt that he and his father were men together. "No man's ignorant that can farm the way you can. No man's ignorant that can train dogs right. But any man that don't know what he can do and has to go to high school to try to find out—that is awful ignorant!"

He stopped talking, suddenly conscious of his father's eyes. They were looking straight into his own with a warm, awakening understanding. "All right," his father said.

They walked on toward the car, keeping step, heads up, feet coming down firmly and rhythmically on the ground.

Home
Is the Hero

Corey Ford

He drew deep breaths, spreading his nostrils and trying to get it better. He remembered it best with his nose. His eyes remembered the gate and the lawn and the white house, but what his nose remembered, as the car turned the corner and started down the wide, familiar street, was the way the asphalt simmered in the noonday heat, the cool-smelling shadows under the maples, the steamy smell of fresh-mown grass on the lawn. He sniffed the air, and his body shivered a little with excitement.

His excitement had been mounting each hour during the long train trip yesterday and, before that, during the trip home across the ocean on the crowded transport. He had never forgotten his home. The thought of it had kept coming back to him at the strangest times: while the guns were blasting and shaking the ground under him, or once on patrol on a dark road in Normandy when a shadow moved and a gutteral command rang in the night. Sometimes in his sleep he would think of coming indoors and tracking mud on the green hall carpet, or hanging around the big, comfortable kitchen while supper was being readied, and his body would twitch and he would make a sobbing sound in his throat. Little things would bring it back—bread baking in a French farmhouse or always the smell of grass in the sun.

The car stopped in front of the house, and he saw them come down the steps and start across the lawn toward him, the man in front, the woman a little behind. The involuntary sobbing began in his throat again, a sharp intake of breath that was like a shrill whisper.

"Hello, Nick," the man said, holding out his hand. "Hello, boy."

He pressed his nose against the man's knuckles, remembering the faint tobacco smell. The sobbing in his throat grew louder, and his tail banged against the sides of the crate. "He knows you," the expressman said.

"Sure he knows me. Don't you, Nick?" He told the expressman, "It's over two years."

"He's quite a dog," the expresssman said admiringly. "I bet he's strong. Lookit the shoulders on him. And those teeth."

"George," the woman said, "now be careful." She was standing a little to the rear of the man, watching uneasily through the pince-nez glasses.

"He's all right, Edie. He's been to detraining school. He's okay." He helped the expressman lift the crate down and set it on the lawn. "Maybe you might have seen his picture in the paper," he mentioned to the expressman.

"Is that who he is"—astonished—"that killed the German? Sure, I was reading about him only the other day."

"He got a decoration for it," the man said with pride. "This German had his pistol pointed, and Nick jumped up and grabbed his wrist, and he got him down and by the throat. It was all in the citation they sent us."

"I'd hate to have him get my throat," the expressman said, slamming the back of the truck.

The woman still hesitated on the lawn with her hands clasped. She was stout, gentle-faced, worried. "George," she said, "do you think you ought to let him out until you're sure . . . ?"

"Sure of what?" The man laughed. He unsnapped the catch and opened the door of the crate. "He wants to stretch his legs."

Nick stepped out of the crate stiffly, his tail whipping against the man's knees. The grass was soft under his feet. His body shook uncontrollably; the excitement was about to burst inside him. He halted for a moment in front of the woman, straining his neck toward her and sniffing. She stood rigid, forcing a weak smile. His nose touched the tip of her fingers, and she snatched her hand away.

"Nick," the man said.

The dog moved past her and let his nose lead him across the lawn to the border of shrubs and along the shrubs to the edge of the porch steps. His tail wagging faster and faster, he sucked the air with long, delicious gasps. His nose was remembering it all: the favorite place behind the steps, the cool hole he used to dig in the dirt under the lilac, the water dish. He followed his nose across the driveway onto the lawn, and he began trotting faster, galloping in a wide circle, halting abruptly to sniff the grass again. He wanted to press his nose deep in it, to feel it against his belly, to lose himself again in the sweet smell of grass in the sun. He rolled onto his side and over onto his back and began to wriggle ecstatically across the lawn, kicking his legs and arching his powerful neck to inch himself forward. He twisted first one way and then the other like a puppy, making deep growls, sneezing.

"Glad to be out of the Army?" The man laughed, and he laughed back, his tongue lolling and his strong white teeth showing. The woman caught her breath as he squirmed off the edge of the lawn into a border of flowers.

"George," she wailed, "he's ruining the iris."

The man called, "Nick!" and he rose and shook himself and trotted over, tail slapping. "Come on, boy. Let's go in the house and say hello to Richie."

"You're not going to let him in the house?"

"Why not? Of course."

"But you don't know how he'll be with Richie. He's apt as not to . . . ." She did not finish the sentence.

"Edie, he isn't apt to anything. He's the same as he always was. He went away to war and now he's back, that's all."

"But suppose something happened, George. After all, he's been trained to . . . ." She had a way of letting her sentences trail off into significant silence.

Reluctantly he yielded. "I'll keep a rope on him at first."

The dog sat still as the man knelt and slipped a rope

through his collar. He rested one forepaw on the man's knee.

"This way, boy."

He knew the way himself. He tugged up the front-porch steps ahead of the man, through the vestibule that smelled nostalgically of overshoes and garden tools and a worn doormat, and through the door into the front hall. Instantly the dank remembered darkness swallowed him—the newel post, the big mahogany hat rack, the clock. A chewed leather glove that he used to play with lay on the green carpet beside the clock, and he sniffed at it as he went by. He paused and sniffed again suspiciously. There was a strange, unremembered smell about the glove, the smell of another dog.

"Here, Nick," the man said, leading him into the living room. "Where's Richie?" He raised his voice. "Oh, Richie!"

Descending feet thumped on the staircase, and his ears pointed forward stiffly. The little whistling sob began again in his throat, growing louder and louder. The footsteps pounded along the hall, and a five-year-old boy burst through the door and flung himself toward him, arms outstretched.

"Richard!" The woman's voice rang with alarm. The boy halted abruptly. "Just don't get too near him, honey."

The boy stood uncertainly in the doorway, his smile fading, his questioning eyes going to his mother's face and back to the dog.

Nick was straining at the rope, pulling so hard that his collar choked him. He wanted to rush to the boy, to lap his face over, to feel the boy's fist clutch his fur as he hugged him. He belonged to Richie; he had always been

Richie's dog. He had shadowed him morning and night, had stood beside his carriage when Richie was too young to walk, had slept on a blanket beside Richie's crib. They had wrestled together, and he had carried Richie on his back, and at night they had stretched out before the fireplace and Richie had gone to sleep with his head on a shaggy shoulder. He stood on his hind legs at the end of the rope, pawing the air and whimpering shrilly.

"Easy, Nick," the man said. "Easy.'"

The strain of the rope was pulling his lips back, baring his white teeth. The boy moved backward a step, watching him.

"Say hello to Nick," the man prompted.

A yelp, a wild scrambling, a flash of golden brown, and a small toy spaniel darted past Richie's legs and slid to a halt before Nick, snarling and snapping hysterically. The fur rose along Nick's backbone; a rumble started deep in his chest. The spaniel's barking rose to a scream, and he ran back to Richie, leaping up onto him and whimpering. Richie gathered him in his arms and held him tight. He faced the big dog with a gathering pucker between his eyes.

The woman said, "You'd better take Scamper back up to your room, Richard, before he . . . ."

Richie hugged the wriggling spaniel, stroking his head to soothe him. He turned and started back toward the stairs.

"There." She spoke with a sharp exhalation of breath. "George, you'll have to do something. He can't stay in the house tonight. It makes me too nervous."

"But where will he stay?"

"I don't know. The garage, I suppose. I wouldn't sleep

a wink," she said, her stout, sweet face lined with worry. "I'd be thinking about . . . ." Her pince-nez glasses bobbed as she shook her head. "Once they've learned to . . . ." She let the sentence trail.

He walked quietly beside the man out of the house, down the steps, and across the lawn. He followed dutifully as the man led him through the garage doors and across the cool oil-soaked cement floor and made his rope fast in the spare room behind the garage. The man took a blanket from the car. He watched him with questioning eyes as he spread it on the floor. He could not believe it was for him.

The man hesitated a moment, and then walked over and knelt beside him. "Sorry, Nick," he murmured, working his fingers deep into the fur behind the dog's ears and scratching him. "It's not much of a homecoming, boy, but . . . ." The man's fingers slid along his neck and down his solid ribs, smoothing his fur. "It'll be all right," the man said vaguely, and patted his flank. He rose slowly. "It'll be all right tomorrow."

He watched in silence as the man walked out of the room and closed the door behind him. Still, he could not believe it. He crouched on the blanket with his head resting on his forepaws, watching the door. He made no effort to whine or bark. In the Army you are taught to be quiet. You don't make a sound; you don't even whimper.

That night the man brought some food and water, and then he went out and shut the door again. Nick lay silent, trying to understand what he had done. He remembered his bed on the floor in Richie's room, and he tried to think why he was not there. Wondering, he fell asleep, and in his sleep he was walking down a dark road in Normandy.

A soldier was walking beside him, his pants tucked into the tops of a dusty pair of combat boots, his webbed cartridge belt sagging from a hip. They moved in silence, he and the young soldier, listening for a sound in the night. There was an effortless understanding between the soldier and himself, a sort of mutual homelessness. They were alone, the two of them, against the dark night. The soldier needed him, needed his nose to smell danger, needed his ears to hear.

Then ahead of them Nick saw the shadow move again, he saw the arm lift with the pistol pointing, and in his sleep he began to jerk convulsively. His legs scratched the cement floor of the garage as he tried to leap; his jaws champed together. He woke with a start and stared wildly for a moment at the strange blackness around him before he remembered he was home.

In the morning the door opened. He was on his feet, tail wagging expectantly. Richie peered cautiously inside and beckoned over his shoulder; a group of neighbors' children followed him, staring at Nick.

"There he is. See?" Richie said. His voice was shrill with importance.

Nick tugged at the rope, panting. His teeth gleamed. "He looks just like a wolf," a tall girl said, shivering pleasantly.

"He killed a German," Richie said. "He killed about a hundred Germans, I guess. He ate all their heads off."

"I got a brother in the Marines," a boy said.

"Can I pet him?" asked a little boy, holding the tall girl's hand.

"Oh, no, you can't touch him," Richie said. "My mother said not to. You can watch while I feed him, though."

The group edged into the room in fascinated silence. Richie took a chunk of meat from a pan in his hand and tossed it to Nick. It fell short. He took a stick and poked the chunk across the floor within his reach.

"He didn't eat it," the little boy said after a moment, disappointed.

"Here, Nick," Richie said, and poked the chunk of meat nearer. He stepped back quickly.

Nick still ignored the meat. His eyes were on Richie's face, his throat was making the little sobbing sound again. This wasn't the way it used to be when Richie would toss a baseball to him, and he would bring it back and put his paws on Richie's shoulders and knock him down, and Richie would laugh.

"Look, Scamper's eating it instead," the little boy announced.

The spaniel had sneaked unnoticed past the group. He darted across the garage floor, seized the meat, and turned to run. It happened before they knew it. Soundlessly Nick lunged and grabbed him, shook him once, and tossed him in the air. The spaniel landed at Richie's feet, howling and snapping at a spreading red stain on his golden-brown fur. Nick lunged again, but the rope snubbed him short, half turning him.

The children ran out of the garage, their screams blending with the spaniel's shrieks of pain. Richie's eyes were blinded with tears. Furiously he ran at Nick and struck him across the face with the stick. He stooped, picked up the spaniel, and carried him wailing into the house.

Later Nick heard the car start, and hours later he heard it come back. He could hear Richie crying as his mother led him into the house. He waited, shaking convulsively.

He was confused; everything confused him. He was home, but home wasn't here. Home wasn't having people come and stare at you and always keeping a little distance from you. Home was jumping up on a cot and having your stomach rubbed and smelling chicken frying on the barracks stove. Home was somebody's field jacket beside a pair of GI shoes on the floor. Home was marching together and sharing out of the same mess kit and crawling under a shelter half together in the rain. Home was anywhere you were together. . . .

Sometime later he heard another car stop in front of the house, and he recognized the man's voice. He stood erect and began to pant. The woman was talking to the man. He could hear her voice rising and falling as they walked toward the garage.

". . . seven stitches. The veterinarian said he'd have to stay there at least a week. Richie's upstairs, poor child. He's all upset. I put him to bed, and then I phoned you. He said the dog simply grabbed little Scamper without any warning."

They had halted in the doorway of the garage. He could see the woman's pince-nez glasses blink. "It's what I kept telling you all along."

"Nick, Nick," the man said unhappily, looking through the door at him.

"I was afraid when they first wrote they were sending him back," the woman said. "I didn't want him to come."

"But, Edie, this is his home. You couldn't refuse to take him back after he did his job and even got a decoration for it—"

"For what? For killing. Oh, I know he was a hero,

George, but why did he have to come home again? Why didn't he die a hero over there?"

The man stared at her, shocked. The intensity of her feeling was bringing out unaccustomed sharp lines in her plump face. Fear made her that way, he realized; she was deathly afraid. "He didn't mean it, Edie," he said. "It was a mistake. Maybe seeing Richie with a new dog. He was always such a pet."

"Pet!" She let out her breath so sharply that her whole body yanked erect. She controlled herself. "I know it isn't his fault, George, but the Army's made him brutal." Her face was sharp. "How could you ever trust him again after . . . ?"

The man walked over thoughtfully and stood beside Nick. The dog did not tug at the rope. He waited, looking up at the man's face. He was still shaking, his loins contracted, his back arched high.

"Nick," the man said experimentally. "Look, Nick." He held out his hand. "Roll over," he said.

He began to pant louder, looking up at the man. He knew it was a command, but he could not remember what it was. He was confused, things were rushing through his mind. He could hear the guns again and the creak of leather and the thud of feet marching. He could hear them above everything else, above his own panting.

"Nick," the man pleaded, "don't you remember? Roll over, boy."

It was a command, and he knew he was supposed to do something, but he was too mixed up now to know what. Everything was mixed up. This wasn't home; he wasn't home anymore. Home was a pair of high-topped combat boots and a sagging cartridge belt and a young soldier walking beside him down a dark road in Normandy.

"Roll over," the man said again sharply, and snapped his fingers.

He heard the click of a pistol being cocked, and he saw an outstretched arm. He leaped and grabbed the wrist in his teeth.

The man stood looking at the round drops of blood on his wrist, with a surprised, almost sheepish smile. He wrapped a handkerchief around his wrist. "He didn't mean it," he was saying apologetically.

The woman's voice suddenly went all to pieces. "There's only one thing to do. He'll have to be put away."

"But he didn't mean it."

"I'm going to phone the authorities. They can come and get him."

The man hesitated as she hurried toward the house. The big dog was cowering, ears back and tail hugging his flanks. The man knelt beside him and scratched above his neck.

"I understand. I remember after the last war," he murmured. "I remember how it was when I came home." He was fumbling with the dog's collar. "Good-by, boy," he said, and rose and walked quickly toward the house.

Nick took a step forward. The rope slid from his collar and fell to the floor. He walked out of the garage; he did not run. He walked across the lawn and out through the gate without looking back. He walked down the maple-shaded street, and he did not look back as he turned the corner.

He crossed the street and started through the park, through the cool-smelling grass. A stranger was sitting on a bench, reading a newspaper. He had on a new gray civilian suit, but on his outstretched feet was a pair of battered Army shoes, dark with dust. Nick paused, sniffing the familiar smell of leather and shoe polish.

The stranger lowered the paper and looked at him. "Beat it," he said, and returned to the paper.

Nick sat on his haunches and waited. The stranger tore the want-ad section out of the paper and stuffed it into his pocket. Nick rose to his feet, ready. The stranger looked at him again and shook his head.

"Look," he said, reaching out a hand and scratching him absently behind an ear, "I'd take you home, but I haven't got any home to take you to. So beat it. . . ."

He paused, feeling the ear and frowning. He bent the ear toward him and looked at Nick's Army serial number branded on the inside of it. "You and me both, eh?" he said slowly.

He got up and started walking, whistling. Nick walked beside him into the dusk.

Dog Star *Arthur C. Clarke*

When I heard Laika's frantic barking, my first reaction
was one of annoyance. I turned over in my bunk and
murmured sleepily, "Shut up, you silly bitch." That dreamy
interlude lasted only a fraction of a second; then con-
sciousness returned, and with it fear. Fear of loneliness
and fear of madness.

For a moment I dared not open my eyes; I was afraid
of what I might see. Reason told me that no dog had ever
set foot upon this world, that Laika was separated from
me by a quarter of a million miles of space and, far more
irrevocably, five years of time.

"You've been dreaming," I told myself angrily. "Stop being a fool. Open your eyes! You won't see anything except the glow of the wall paint."

That was right, of course. The tiny cabin was empty, the door tightly closed. I was alone with my memories, overwhelmed by the transcendental sadness that often comes when some bright dream fades into drab reality. The sense of loss was so desolating that I longed to return to sleep. It was well that I failed to do so, for at that moment sleep would have been death. But I did not know this for another five seconds, and during that eternity I was back on Earth, seeking what comfort I could from the past.

No one ever discovered Laika's origin, though the Observatory staff made a few inquiries and I inserted several advertisements in the Pasadena newspapers. I found her, a lost and lonely ball of fluff, huddled by the roadside one summer evening when I was driving up to Palomar. Though I have never liked dogs, or indeed any animals, it was impossible to leave this helpless little creature to the mercy of the passing cars. With some qualms, wishing that I had a pair of gloves, I picked her up and dumped her in the baggage compartment. I was not going to hazard the upholstery of my new '92 Vik and felt that she could do little damage there. In this, I was not altogether correct.

When I had parked the car at the Monastery—the astronomers' residential quarters where I'd be living for the next week—I inspected my find without much enthusiasm. At that stage, I had intended to hand the puppy over to the janitor, but then it whimpered and opened its eyes. There was such an expression of helpless trust in them that— Well, I changed my mind.

Sometimes I regretted that decision, though never for long. I had no idea how much trouble a growing dog could cause, deliberately and otherwise. My cleaning and repair bills soared; I could never be sure of finding an unravaged pair of socks or an unchewed copy of the *Astrophysical Journal*. But eventually Laika was both house-trained and Observatory-trained; she must have been the only dog ever to be allowed inside the two-hundred-inch dome. She would lie there quietly in the shadows for hours while I was up in the cage making adjustments, quite content if she could hear my voice from time to time. The other astronomers became equally fond of her (it was old Dr. Anderson who suggested her name), but from the beginning she was my dog and would obey no one else. Not that she would always obey me.

She was a beautiful animal, about 95 percent Alsatian. It was that missing 5 percent, I imagine, that led to her being abandoned. (I still feel a surge of anger when I think of it, but since I shall never know the facts, I may be jumping to false conclusions.) Apart from two dark patches over the eyes, most of her body was a smoky gray, and her coat was soft as silk. When her ears were pricked up, she looked incredibly intelligent and alert; sometimes I would be discussing spectral types or stellar evolution with my colleagues, and it would be hard to believe that she was not following the conversation.

Even now I cannot understand why she became so attached to me, for I have made very few friends among human beings. Yet when I returned to the Observatory after an absence, she would go almost frantic with delight, bouncing around on her hind legs and putting her paws on my shoulders—which she could reach quite easily

—all the while uttering small squeaks of joy, which seemed highly inappropriate from so large a dog. I hated to leave her for more than a few days at a time, and though I could not take her with me on overseas trips, she accompanied me on most of my shorter journeys. She was with me when I drove north to attend that ill-fated seminar at Berkeley.

We were staying with university acquaintances; they had been polite about it, but obviously did not look forward to having a monster in the house. However, I assured them that Laika never gave the slightest trouble, and rather reluctantly they let her sleep in the living room. "You needn't worry about burglars tonight," I said.

"We don't have any in Berkeley," they answered, rather coldly.

In the middle of the night, it seemed that they were wrong. I was awakened by a hysterical, high-pitched barking from Laika that I had heard only once before, when she had first seen a cow and did not know what on earth to make of it. Cursing, I threw off the sheets and stumbled out into the darkness of the unfamiliar house. My main thought was to silence Laika before she roused my hosts, assuming that it was not already far too late. If there had been an intruder, he would certainly have taken flight by now. Indeed, I rather hoped that he had.

For a moment I stood beside the switch at the top of the stairs, wondering whether to throw it. Then I growled, "Shut up, Laika!" and flooded the place with light.

She was scratching frantically at the door, pausing from time to time to give that hysterical yelp. "If you want out," I said angrily, "there's no need for all that fuss."

I went down, shot the bolt, and she took off into the night like a rocket.

It was very calm and still, with a waning moon struggling to pierce the San Francisco fog. I stood in the luminous haze, looking out across the water to the lights of the city, waiting for Laika to come back so that I could chastise her suitably. I was still waiting when, for the second time in the twentieth century, the San Andreas Fault woke from its sleep.

Oddly enough, I was not frightened—at first. I can remember that two thoughts passed through my mind in the moment before I realized the danger. Surely, I told myself, the geophysicists could have given us *some* warning. And then I found myself thinking, with great surprise, I'd no idea that earthquakes make so much noise!

It was about then that I knew that this was no ordinary quake. What happened afterward, I would prefer to forget. The Red Cross did not take me away until quite late the next morning because I refused to leave Laika. As I looked at the shattered house containing the bodies of my friends, I knew that I owed my life to her; but the helicopter pilots could not be expected to understand that, and I cannot blame them for thinking that I was crazy, like so many of the others they had found wandering among the fires and the debris.

After that, I do not suppose we were ever apart for more than a few hours. I have been told, and I can well believe it, that I became less and less interested in human company without being actively unsocial or misanthropic. Between them, the stars and Laika filled all my needs. We used to go for long walks together over the mountains. It was the happiest time I have ever known. There was only one flaw; I knew, though Laika could not, how soon it must end.

We had been planning the move for more than a decade. As far back as the 1960's it was realized that Earth was no place for an astronomical observatory. Even the small pilot instruments on the moon had far outperformed all the telescopes peering through the murk and haze of the terrestrial atmosphere. The story of Mount Wilson, Palomar, Greenwich, and the other names was coming to an end. They would still be used for training purposes, but the research frontier must move out into space.

I had to move with it; indeed, I had already been offered the post of deputy director, Farside Observatory. In a few months, I could hope to solve problems I had been working on for years. Beyond the atmosphere I would be like a blind man who had suddenly been given sight.

It was utterly impossible, of course, to take Laika with me. The only animals on the moon were those needed for experimental purposes. It might be another generation before pets were allowed, and even then it would cost a fortune to carry them there and to keep them alive. Providing Laika with her usual two pounds of meat a day would take, I calculated, several times my quite comfortable salary.

The choice was simple and straightforward. I could stay on Earth and abandon my career. Or I could go to the moon and abandon Laika.

After all, she was only a dog. In a dozen years she would be dead, while I should be reaching the peak of my profession. No sane man would have hesitated over the matter. Yet I did hesitate, and if by now you do not understand why, no further words of mine can help.

In the end I let matters go by default. Up to the very week I was due to leave I had still made no plans for Laika. When Dr. Anderson volunteered to look after her, I accepted numbly, with scarcely a word of thanks. The old physicist and his wife had always been fond of her, and I am afraid they considered me indifferent and heartless, when the truth was just the opposite. We went for one more walk together over the hills; then I delivered her silently to the Andersons and did not see her again.

Takeoff was delayed almost twenty-four hours until a major flare storm had cleared the Earth's orbit; even so, the Van Allen belts were still so active that we had to make our exit through the North Polar Gap. It was a miserable flight. Apart from the usual trouble with weightlessness, we were all groggy with antiradiation drugs. The ship was already over Farside before I took much interest in the proceedings, so I missed the sight of Earth dropping below the horizon. Nor was I really sorry; I wanted no reminders and intended to think only of the future. Yet I could not shake off that feeling of guilt. I had deserted someone who loved and trusted me and was no better than those who had abandoned Laika when she was a puppy, beside the dusty road to Palomar.

The news that she was dead reached me a month later. There was no reason that anyone knew; the Andersons had done their best and were very upset. She had just lost interest in living, it seemed. For a while, I think I did the same, but work is a wonderful anodyne, and my program was just getting under way. Though I never forgot Laika, in a little while the memory ceased to hurt.

Then why had it come back to haunt me, five years later, on the far side of the moon? I was searching my mind for the reason when the metal building around me quivered as if under the impact of a heavy blow. I reacted without thinking and was already closing the helmet of my emergency suit when the foundations slipped and the wall tore open with a short-lived scream of escaping air. Because I had automatically pressed the general-alarm button we lost only two men, despite the fact that the tremor, the worst ever recorded on Farside, cracked all three of the Observatory's pressure domes.

It is hardly necessary for me to say that I do not believe in the supernatural. Everything that happened has a perfectly rational explanation, obvious to any man with the slightest knowledge of psychology. In the second San Francisco earthquake, Laika was not the only dog to sense approaching disaster; many such cases were reported. And on Farside, my own memories must have given me that heightened awareness, when my never-sleeping subconscious detected the first faint vibrations from within the moon.

The human mind has strange and labyrinthine ways of going about its business; it knew the signal that would most swiftly rouse me to the knowledge of danger. There is nothing more to it than that. Though in a sense one could say that Laika woke me on both occasions, there is no mystery about it, no miraculous warning across the gulf that neither man nor dog can ever bridge.

Of that I am sure, if I am sure of anything. Yet sometimes I wake now, in the silence of the moon, and wish that the dream could have lasted a few seconds longer so that I could have looked just once more into those luminous brown eyes, brimming with an unselfish, un-demanding love I have found nowhere else on this or on any other world.

The Little Red Chair

Helen Ellwanger Hanford

From where I sat in Ellman's comfortable living room a
glint of bright color in the corner caught my eye, and I
left the group by the fire and strolled over to investigate.
I found that I had been looking at a tiny chair painted
a brilliant red. It was obviously handmade, and rather
clumsily at that, yet with a certain care that suggested
unskilled but loving workmanship. I guessed that it had
been intended either for a very small child or a rather
large doll.

"Bring it over," invited Ellman, and turning to the
others he added, "I've had that little chair since I was a

baby and it's all tied up with a very curious experience that my mother and I had when I was six years old." We urged him to tell us the story.

"It's a queer thing," he said, "and of course I know in advance what you'll make of it, but I thought something quite different forty years ago, and I'll have to admit I do still sometimes when I wake up before morning and can't get back to sleep.

"We were living, my father and mother and I, on a small farm in western New York. My father was a nursery-man, but he also grew fine fruit for the market. It was late in August, in the very heart of the fruit season, and Early Crawfords were ripe and Harvest apples and round purple plums—I forget their name.

"He meant to drive to Rochester, fifteen miles away, and dispose of his fruit. Then he had some important business to attend to that might take another day to finish up. The question was whether he should come back that night and later make a second trip, or should he put up at the old Whitcomb House and return the next night.

"He never left us when he could help it. Our farm was isolated, and my mother was a city-bred woman; he always hated to leave her alone at night.

"My mother, young and slender with masses of brown hair and gentle dark eyes, was hiding her fears if she had any and was trying to argue him out of his. 'You can't afford to give another day to it,' she urged. 'Besides, Willie is going to take care of me. Aren't you, Willie?'

"I assumed a militant attitude, and my father gave me a reluctant, 'Well—' Then he said good-by to me, kissed my mother again, and drove out of the yard.

"I remember it seemed very quiet and lonesome there

in the early morning without his big, kindly presence. I think my mother felt it too for she was silent as we walked slowly around the house to the elm-tree seat.

"Susie the cat, trailed by her six kittens, came and lay down at our feet and my mother stroked her with gentle hand. I loved Susie dearly but not with my whole heart. That had been given to a little fox terrier that had grown up with me and that had met a tragic death over a year before.

"Dandy, I believe, was his real name, but as a baby I had heard my father say, 'Come, little dog,' 'Here, little dog,' and had supposed that was his name. So Little Dog he became, a funny, alert little chap with one brown ear always cocked and an absurd habit of standing in front of us and barking most terribly at strangers and then, when he had won them over or had been assured that they were harmless, of running back and putting his head in our laps.

"All that was loving and sweet natured Little Dog was, and when that summer day he was found stiff and cold it was a real grief to my parents. They had never told me of his death, so I supposed he had wandered off as he sometimes did and still dreamed of his happy return.

"Finally my mother pushed back her pretty hair and stood up. 'I've got to work now, Willie,' she said, and started toward the side porch. I followed unwillingly, not wanting her to be out of my sight and yet hating the house on this lovely morning. I kept close at her heels as she went about her work. At last when she had tripped over me for the tenth time she laughed and considered. 'Here's a job for you, Willie,' she said. 'Come out on the porch.'

"I sat down at the porch table where my mother often worked in the morning, and she brought out silver polish and cloths and then a rack full of knives and forks and spoons.

"'The lamb cake dish too,' I begged. 'Bring out everything.'

"My mother smiled, and from the cupboard where they were kept she got out the high cake dish with the fascinating little lamb on the handle, and the big, old platter with the grapes running around it that Grandma Ellman used to have, and finally the tea and coffee service that they gave Grandpa Walter when he had preached twenty-five years. To my mind it all made a great showing, and I sat there surrounded by my treasures and going happily from one thing to another without actually finishing anything.

"It must have been noon when the interruption came. I heard the creak of the front gate and ran to the edge of the porch to see who it was. In a minute a most disreputable-looking man came around the corner of the house. His face under his battered hat was red and heavy-looking, with a stubbly black beard all over it. Over one shoulder he carried a bundle on the end of a stick. He was looking toward the dog kennel where Little Dog had used to live. Then he caught sight of me.

"'Got a dog?' he asked.

"'No,' I confessed sorrowfully. 'Little Dog's gone.'

"'Little Dog—huh!' He came up to the porch and stood still for a minute looking at my gleaming array. Then he sat down heavily on the step.

"'Pa at home?' was his next question.

"With the eagerness of the young to give information I

told him my father's plans in detail. 'He won't be back till tomorrow probably,' I finished. 'I'm taking care of my mother.'

" 'Ye are, are ye?' he said with a laugh, and at the sight of his yellow teeth—broken off, some of them—and at something in his face I didn't quite understand, I began to feel a little uncomfortable.

"But by that time my mother, never away from me for very long, was in the doorway.

"The tramp stood up. 'I'm looking for work, ma'am,' he said.

" 'I'm afraid I haven't any work for you,' said my mother, 'and my husband isn't at home just now.'

"It sounded as if he might be back almost any minute, and I thought how queer it was for her to put it that way. The man looked at her and grinned.

"My mother flushed, but her steady gaze did not falter. 'If you are hungry,' she said, 'I can give you some lunch.'

"She put the silver aside and set a place at the end of the table. Then, moving about lightly, she brought out cold meat and bread, doughnuts and coffee, and told the man to sit down. I did not take my eyes off him once as he ate. He finished.

" 'Thank you, ma'am,' he called loudly to my mother, and to me, 'I guess I'll be going.' But he didn't go. He stood, stretching his arms and looking from me and my silver to the kitchen doorway. One of the kittens crawled up close, and as he shifted from one foot to the other he came down on the little creature's paw. It gave a sharp mew of pain, and instantly Susie was upon him digging into his legs with her sharp claws. With an oath he flung her off into the yard.

" 'Oh, for shame!' cried my mother, running out.

"As for me, I flew at him in a rage. 'Don't you dare hurt my cat!' I screamed.

"He caught hold of me and held me at arm's length, pinching me a little under the arms as he did so. He felt terribly strong and I suddenly wanted to cry, but before any of us could say or do anything more we heard the sound of wagon wheels in the distance. A great load of hay was coming along the road. His look changed, and I wasn't afraid of him anymore. He set me down hastily, seized his bundle, backed off the porch, and walked out of the yard, not toward the road but southwest, past the barn and over the wire fence, going across lots.

"It was the Bateses on the hay wagon, just as I'd thought. They lived half a mile up the road. Grandpa Bates, as I called him, an old man over eighty, sat placidly watching the road ahead, but his son saw us at once and drew up. My mother gave a quick glance back. The tramp was just disappearing down the slope. To my surprise, my mother said nothing of our visitor, and apparently the two men had not noticed him as they drove along.

" 'How is Mrs. Bates?' my mother asked instead. 'Wait a minute. I have some jelly for her.'

"I stood staring at the Bateses and finally—my mother seemed very slow in coming out—Grandpa Bates returned from that far-off place where old men sit and chew straws and looked at me kindly.

" 'Hello, Willie,' Grandpa Bates said in his high, old voice, 'how's your little doggie?'

" 'Why, don't you remember?' I asked. 'He ran away.'

" 'Of course, to be sure. Well, don't you fret, Willie. He'll be turning up one of these days like a bad penny.'

" 'Why didn't you tell them about poor Susie?' I asked reproachfully when the Bateses had gone.

" 'We mustn't bother other people,' said my mother. 'Not when it isn't necessary. The man's gone now, Willie. It's all right.'

"We walked back to the porch and my mother slowly gathered up the silver and we washed it and put it away. Then we went out again and sat down. Susie limped up presently and joined us.

" 'Mother,' I whispered, 'I'm sorry for Susie and I do love her, but I wish Little Dog would come back.'

" 'I know,' she said comfortingly, and after a minute she added soberly, 'I wish we had a good watchdog. We need one here.'

" 'Everything's spoiled now,' I said at last.

" 'No, no!' cried my mother. 'Why, whatever are we thinking of, Willie? It's dinner time. I tell you, let's have it in the grape arbor for a change, shall we?'

"It was well on in the afternoon and we had put away our dinner things and I, for one, had had a nap when I heard my mother give an exclamation of surprise. I looked up and saw—but I'll tell you how she always described it later.

"She saw an animal coming the road, trotting soberly along. As it came nearer she could see that it was a huge dog of a breed with which she was not familiar, though it had something of the heaviness and nobility of the Saint Bernard. Dusty and travel stained, it paused at the open gate and then turned in and came straight toward us.

" 'Mother?' I cried in delight. 'Oh, where did he come from?'

" 'Why, I can't imagine,' said my mother. 'Be a little

careful, Willie.' Then as he stood quietly, looking from one to another of us with good eyes, she patted his head tentatively. 'Nice dog! Maybe he'll stay.'

"I was prancing around him. 'Come, Little Dog! Come, Little Dog!' I called.

"The idea of calling anything so huge by that name made my mother laugh but she reasoned that in my mind Little Dog had become the generic name for dog, so she said nothing. She never spoiled little things for me.

" 'Hungry, doggie?' she asked. 'Come,' and she put food and a basin of water on the side porch. He did not touch the food, but the water he lapped up gratefully.

" 'Now I suppose he'll go,' said my mother.

"I looked up at her. It seemed the strangest thing to say. 'Oh, but Mother, we'd never let him!' I said earnestly. 'I'd hold him.'

"She smiled again at the thought of my puny strength pitted against that of this great creature. 'I wish he would stay,' she said, and she put her hand on his neck. He gave her the clear look of a kind dog and stretched out on the porch with a benevolent glance for the bristling Susie. But I was eager for a romp, 'Come, Little Dog,' I shouted, and my mother smiled to see him get slowly to his feet and go sideways down the steps in answer to my call.

" 'Don't play too hard,' she said. 'He must be tired.'

"So I gave him little intervals of rest between our frolics on that happiest afternoon of all my childhood, and while he rested I asked him innumerable questions, bending close to his ear, and if he did not answer he at least listened and I was satisfied. Over in the arbor my mother sewed. Once I ran to her with a request. 'I want my little red chair,' I said. 'You know, the one Grandpa Bates made for me.'

"My mother looked up from her work. 'Oh, no, Willie, I can't get that. It's put away. You outgrew it long ago.'

" 'No, no,' I insisted. 'Oh, please, Mother, I want to see if—'

"But my mother, who in spite of her gentleness could be very firm, stopped me with a quiet glance that made me remember that I had promised my father not to tease and so I ran away again without finishing my sentence.

"As the sun got low my mother grew very restless. Finally she said, 'Willie, how would you like it for us to spend the night over at the Bateses?'

" 'Oh, Mother,' I cried, 'when maybe Father will come home and bring me a present!'

" 'Yes,' she considered, 'he may come home.' She hesitated. 'Let's see if Little Dog will come into the house.'

" 'Of course he will. Come, Little Dog,' I commanded.

"The dog arose at once, and to my mother's delight lumbered after us into the house. He looked around for a minute, and then he went and lay down by the sofa in the corner of the kitchen with just the faintest wag of his tail. 'Just where Little Dog loved to lie,' my mother said and stood looking at him a moment.

"Then she made up the fire, and we had our supper there on the kitchen table, with a lamp presently to light us for we had stayed out late. Indeed we had done nothing on time all that day.

"After a while, when it was quite dark, my mother got out the big old lantern and fastened it on its hook out on the porch where it would light my father, if by any chance he should come home late. She seemed so big to me then, but I know now how little and slight she was and scarcely more than a girl as she stood there, hanging up for all the world to see the sign that we were alone that night.

" 'I don't think he will come,' she said, 'but he just might.'

"Then we went in and barred the door—the catch on the screen door was broken, I remember—and after that almost immediately we went upstairs to bed. The dog followed us closely, and to my surprise my mother let him into her room, where he settled himself on the rug at the foot of the bed. She meanwhile locked the door, we undressed quickly and blew out the light, and my mother took me in bed with her. It seemed wonderfully cozy, all three of us there together. It needed only the presence of Susie and her six to make it quite perfect.

"I mentioned the cat family to my mother, and with her laughing protest in my ears I fell asleep. She lay awake for an hour or so listening for the welcome sound of wheels on the road, but at last, worn out by her long day, she too slept.

"At midnight my mother woke up, dreaming that my father had come home and was at the door. She raised herself up to listen, and sure enough she heard a step on the porch. Dazed with sleep, all the events of the day wiped out by the hour of unconsciousness and only the dream remaining, she sprang out of bed. As she reached the bedroom door and found it locked, some sinister thought tried to force its way out, some memory warned her, but vaguely, too vaguely. She groped her way down the stairs, and running to the door she turned the key and pulled back the bolt.

"'William!' she cried, 'Oh, William—' Then she screamed and the sound woke even me.

"I stumbled down to the kitchen. There in the middle of the room was my mother, her hand at her throat; in the doorway against the light of the lantern stood the tramp. For years in nightmares I saw him standing there, gigantic in the frame of the door, and yet that indelible picture lasted no more than a flash. Before my eyes the look on the man's face changed from that evil for which I had no name to an expression of horror, frantic, incredulous horror. With a movement almost unbelievably swift he turned and dashed out onto the porch—just as something leaped past me with a hoarse, roaring sound. I saw the man borne down by a form monstrous and shadowy that battled madly with him in the flickering light of the lantern; I heard his scream of fear and pain and my mother's wild cry, 'Come back! Come back, Little Dog!'

"And then on the porch all was clear once more. Little Dog was standing, his head turned back to us, and the tramp was clattering down the steps. I felt freed at last from the awful spell that had kept me standing there alone. I ran to my mother, and she gathered me in her arms and sank to the floor, her breath coming in great shuddering gasps. Never had I been so terrified. For a while I cried loudly, hiding my face in her shoulder. But when finally the plunging steps died away in the distance my sobs lessened, and when I heard a quick rush of feet and felt a soft head pushing close to me, when looking down I saw the dog's kind eyes, my hardy child's nerves asserted themselves.

"'Look, Mother,' I cried exultantly, 'Little Dog's just

the same. He hasn't forgotten a thing. See how he puts his head in your lap after he has scared them away. Oh, please, please get the little red chair and just see if he won't jump in and curl up the way he used to do! You'll find he hasn't outgrown it!' "

Ellman looked around at us as we bent toward him. "And at that," he said slowly, "my mother opened her eyes and looked down, with the strangest look, as if with a supreme effort she were trying . . . not so much to see as to adjust her vision. I believe that in that instant her world rocked about her as she stared with straining eyes at a thing that could not be.

" 'Little Dog!' she whispered.

"The dog returned her gaze steadily, but I saw one ear go up as though he heard some sound. Then he lifted his head gently from her lap and took a step back.

" 'Mother,' I whispered, 'don't let him go.'

"My mother heard and tried to put out her hand, but it fell limply to her side.

"For just one moment at the door Little Dog paused and our eyes met. I knew then that he was not mine to keep. 'Good-by, Little Dog,' I sobbed and turned to my mother.

"When I looked up again she and I were alone once more. From the darkness outside came the creak of wagon wheels and my father's cheerful hail."

The Honor
of the County *Walter D. Edmonds*

I was a proud boy that morning, marching up the lane
with the bull terrier at my heels. It was the spring of the
year and we were just up from New York, and a friend
of my father had given me the dog in March. I wanted to
show him to Uncle Ledyard and Doone and Kathy, but
particularly I wanted to show him to John Callant. John
Callant, I thought, had known something of fighting dogs
in the ring. But, as a matter of politeness, I went first to
the big house.

"Stay there," I commanded the dog when we came to
the office door, for he was well trained, and I wanted to

show him off. He sat down with great dignity, a statue of
white marble on the block of limestone, and pricked his
ears toward the racetrack where John Callant had one of
the colts in harness. His nose worked quietly. I don't
believe he had ever been in really open country before.

I went into the office to find Uncle Ledyard going over
the records of the horses Blue Dandy would be racing that
August at Syracuse. But he dropped everything when
he heard me and swung around on his chair and got up.
His cold eyes smiled at me, and he said in his heavy voice,
"How are you, Teddy? I heard you got back last night.
How's your mother? And father?" And we went through
the family politely and gravely. "Kathy will want to see
you right away."

We went into the living room, and he roared for Kathy.
She entered from the dining room, tall, graciously wel-
coming, and I looked at her curiously, for my mother had
told me that Kathy was going to have a baby this summer. But she didn't seem changed at all, except that her
eyes were quieter.

"Hello, Mister Teddy!" Mrs. Callant cried from the
dining-room door. "How you've growed, to be sure!"

And I said with dignity, "Hello, Mrs. Callant." And
she made me a sign that meant she had fried doughnuts
that morning.

Then Doone came down from his bedroom with his
overalls on, ready to take the horses onto the track, and
we shook hands. I felt that I was back in my own country.
But I was holding my breath with excitement too.

"It's time I was going out," Doone said. "Want to
come along, Teddy?"

"I think I will," I said. And then Doone looked out the

window and saw the dog and said, "Hello, there! Who's that?"

"Oh," I said, "that's my dog. He generally tags after me. And I left him outside. He stays where I tell him to."

"Bring him in," said Uncle Ledyard.

So I went to the office door and whistled, and the dog turned and gravely entered the house. He had great dignity, greeting Uncle Ledyard and Doone, and he put his nose gently into Kathy's lap.

"Oh, Teddy," she said. "He's a beauty! You beautiful dog!"

His ears flattened a little, and his tail waved gently. And Uncle Ledyard said, "He's a fine dog."

And Doone said, "He looks like a good one." And my heart was stuffed with pride.

"What's his name?" said Kathy.

"Leonidas," I said. "For the Spartan."

"That's a fine name for him," said Uncle Ledyard.

Kathy stroked the flat head and said, "My, he's handsome."

Then Artemis, Uncle Ledyard's Gordon setter, entered, and we watched the two dogs greet each other. Leonidas was dignified. He had a grand manner of reserve. After a minute Artemis lost her stiffness, and we saw that they were friends.

We went out to the stable, Doone and I and Leonidas, and John Callant had Blue Dandy harnessed to the sulky, ready to go. He gave me a grin and held the reins while Doone got on the seat, and we watched him from the doors as he jogged the horse out. Leonidas sat on the ramp, taking the sight of the great horse without comment.

"What do you think of him, John?" I asked.

John Callant spat and put his quid back in his cheek and squatted. "Come here," he said to the dog.

Leonidas looked at me and I nodded proudly, and he came stiffly up to John and they looked at each other, the stubby Irishman and the fine white dog with his pointed ears and his deep chest and his steady eyes. The dog posed as if he were on the show bench, and for a moment John stared at him and whistled softly. Then he held out the back of his hand for the dog to sniff, which the dog did, delicately. Then he put his hand under the dog's jaw and drew him gently forward.

John's hands were broad and coarse and stub-fingered, but his touch was like a sculptor's on the white body. It was light and firm and sure with his knowledge of anatomy. The dog closed his eyes, and I saw his muscles playing under the touch.

"He's a brave, handsome beast," said John. "How old is he, and where did you get him, Mister Teddy?"

"He's four years old, and Mr. Freeman, a friend of Father's, gave him to me last winter," I said. "He's pedigreed."

"I've got hands and eyes," said John Callant, "so you needn't be telling me that, Mister Teddy."

There was great respect in John's voice, as if ownership of Leonidas had made me a man's stature.

"There's blood in him to build the finest kingdom in the world," said John, the tone of his speech almost biblical. "And the bull terrier is the king of dogs, the way the lion is the king of beasts."

I squatted down beside him. The morning sun came in

upon us, putting a gold gleam on the short, even white hairs of the dog's coat.

"He's a fighting dog," said John.

"He's got good manners," I said. "He hasn't been any trouble."

"He's no roaring brawler," said John. "But he's fought. You needn't tell me, Mister Teddy. I've handled dogs in me time. He's got the lifting muscles at the back of his head like a bull. Pass your hands down his loin, back of mine. . . . Now over his neck. . . . And now take his jaw in the soft of your hand."

I did as he showed me, and I felt the hard muscles, half asleep, barely stirring at the touch, and my hand thrilled.

"He could whip any dog in the county," said John, "and himself chewing tobacco and a treadmill tied to his tail."

I stiffened, and I looked at Leonidas with a new respect, for whatever John Callant said, I knew he meant. The little man had told me stories of the dog fights on Long Island. And now and then he told stories of the small fights that took place in our valley. And I had heard Uncle Ledyard tell, too, about George Beirne, who was now a white-haired gentleman of sixty-five, but who in the days of his young manhood always had the best dog in the county. He would drive the roads with his dog tailing his cart and stop for any barnyard challenger. And if his own dog was whipped, he would buy the winner from the farmer or fight him if he wouldn't sell. But when Leonidas came into my hands, dog fighting had become an undercover business, and though some of the gentry, as John called them, sometimes attended, they kept the matter to themselves.

And looking at Leonidas now, standing so quietly, it was hard to imagine him in the fury of battle.

"I'm not going to fight him," I said to John Callant. "Father's set against dog fighting."

"To be sure," said John. "You don't want him to be killing all the dogs around here."

I felt virtuously adult, but at the same time a shiver passed through me at his words.

Then Doone called to us from the track to come and hold the watch on Blue Dandy.

The spring went quietly with the voices of the peepers, and I left off fishing for trout and turned my attention to bass. Fishing that summer gave me new pleasure, for everywhere I went Leonidas followed me.

He wasn't a dog given to roughhousing or any form of play. But he walked along beside me on the towpath and lay down in the grass where the bass wouldn't see him, never moving except for his knowledgeful eyes that followed the fly and the occasional prick of his ears toward a rising fish.

But as soon as I struck, he would be on his feet, tense-bodied, his tail trembling stiff and a low, soft, murmuring growl of excitement in his deep chest. And he would be as pleased as I was when the fish was landed.

Or we would depart over the meadows after woodchucks, which he liked better, and he would creep up toward the hole with me and lie flat beside me in the grass—he had far more patience than I at the waiting game—and the moment the woodchuck put his head out and I shot, he would launch himself like a white spear.

But I think best of all, like myself, he enjoyed going

over to Boyd House and watching the horses training
and lying around the cool stalls afterward while John
Callant cleaned the horses of sweat with the smooth strokes
of his stick. He seemed to feel at home in the hot horse
smell with the fresh golden straw wadded between his
forepaws for his chin to rest on, and John Callant would
talk to us as if we were both friends of his.

He was a fine companion for a boy of thirteen, and he
taught me that many things I had been afraid of were
not things to fear at all.

Secret news in our valley travels in a strange way. Halfway through the haying, word came of the drummer and
his dog. He hadn't even crossed the border of Oneida
County, but one morning as John was sponging Blue
Dandy's ears and nostrils, after he had turned in his first
2:07 heat for Doone, he said to me, "Jenkins, the new
drummer for Loftus Company, has got a dog, Mister
Teddy."

"Yes?" I said drowsily, for I was lying on my back under
Blue Dandy's nose, and he was playing with my hand
with his tongue.

"Yes," said John Callant, through his hissing breath.
"I've not heard much about him, but he's whipped the
Belcher dog in Martinsburg."

I didn't answer.

"It means he's pretty good," said John Callant.

There was a rustle in the straw beside me, and Leonidas
dropped his chin into my free hand.

"Well," I said, "I'll bet Leonidas could lick the stuffing
out of him."

"I don't doubt it," said John, and the topic lapsed.

But a week later Adam Fuess, Uncle Ledyard's farmer, dropped into the stable at noon with his after-dinner pipe in his teeth and said, "Well, John, I've just heard the drummer's dog has fixed another."

"Did you?" said John. "He seems to be pretty good."

"Henderson quit before his dog, I heard tell," said Adam. "It took three buckets to get them loose in time."

"He must be a holy terror." And John didn't look at me. Neither man did. They were passing information back and forth.

"Leonidas," I said, annoyed, "could trim him easy."

"Could he?" asked Adam. "This drummer's dog is a trained fighter, I guess."

"John Callant says he could," I said.

John Callant bent down to buckle the belly tab of the blanket. "He ought to," he said, "but I don't know."

"Of course he could," I said, and got up and walked over to the house for my own dinner.

And, as I walked, Leonidas came quietly along beside me, his clean head at my knee and his tail swaying gently. I looked down at him. "You could lick the tar out of him, couldn't you?"

He raised his eyes and pricked his ears, but he didn't lose stride.

During the next week we heard of two dogs beaten, one in Lowville and one in Turin.

The mailman stopped at the barn on his way in and talked to Adam Fuess about it as Adam was cleaning out the manure, and Adam told John, and John told me.

"He killed the second one. They couldn't get him off," said John. "He must be the champion of the world."

The blood rose in my face. "You said yourself Leonidas could beat him!" I cried.

"I said so," said John Callant, "but I don't know, Mister Teddy."

"You do know," I said. "I know, anyway."

"You can't ever tell," said John, "not outside of a ring, that is."

"I won't fight him," I said. "I don't need to. I know."

"Sure and he's your dog entirely," said John placatingly. "But it's a pity there isn't a dog in the valley to stand up to a city slicker."

I don't suppose they knew that they were working on me. To John it was the most natural thing in the world to put one good dog against another. But he had planted his seed carefully the first time he saw the dog, and what he had said since had been no more than careful watering. If you had accused him of putting pressure on me, he would have been hurt. The dog was my dog, and he said so.

But the drummer reached Boonville on the first of August and made his contacts and got his orders. John asked for the evening off, and I knew he was going over to the North American Bar to have a look at the dog. And in spite of myself, I turned up early next morning at Boyd House to hear what he was like.

John Callant was whistling a jig as he cleaned out the stalls and swept the floor. But the rhythm he put into it was speculative and sad. "Hello, Mister Teddy," he said. "Hello, Leonidas, me boy. It's a fine morning."

I sat down on the water bucket and watched the stiff strokes of his broom. He wasn't paying any attention to us that morning, and he worked harder than usual. He raised the chaff dust in clouds, and the horses had their heads over the door with a look in their eyes that was very close to amusement.

"Stand over, will ye, ye great bison!" he roared, when Blue Dandy made a pass at his hat. I laughed. And he whirled around at me and the dog, who was staring outdoors by my feet.

"Oh," said John Callant, "you're there, are you? I thought you had gone."

"Did you see the drummer's dog?" I asked.

"Yes, I saw him. And a fine animal he is too. But I forget, ye aren't interested in him."

"You know that's a lie," I said.

"Oh, it's a liar I am now! Well, you aren't the first one to miscall me in this place."

"That's another," I said.

John grinned and leaned on his broom. "Well, there's plenty of others besides yourself, Mister Teddy."

"What was the dog like?"

"Sure and he's a bull terrier like yours," said John. "Only he has one half a black saddle on his back and one black ear. And he's bigger than yours, and a handsome dog. I don't know that he's handsomer, for he has some scars. But the breeding's in him. I've nothing against the dog," said John Callant, poking his broom at a straw, "but the drummer's not to my taste at all."

"What's the matter with him?"

"Oh, he's kind of a high-and-mighty cuss with a mean look, like sweat in his eye. He stood up to the bar among us and said it was too bad there wasn't any more good dogs to be had in the country parts at all."

"He hasn't seen Leonidas," I said complacently.

John won me by saying, "I told him that meself, Mister Teddy."

"What did he say?"

"Oh, he laughed. He said he was hearing that in considerable towns nowadays, but he wasn't getting a look at the dogs it was said of. He laughed a little, and the boys weren't feeling very friendly about it. 'Talk,' he says. 'I'm a man that knows me manners,' he says, 'but I'm not saying I'll believe it till I see the puppy and the money in his teeth,' he says. 'Well,' he says, 'I suppose the cows are holding out on you boys, and the money's hard to give away.'"

John began to sweep again slowly, now and then casting a surreptitious glance at Leonidas. "The trouble, according to the drummer, was that there wasn't any more decent-bred dogs in the country parts," said John. "Or if there was, their owners was too cowardly to let the brave dogs fight."

"I'm not," I said. "It's just I don't want to."

"That's what I told the drummer," said John. "But he laughed at me, and some of the boys laughed too."

"You know Leonidas could lick him!" I cried, feeling my fists get hot and the tears in my head.

"Sure I do. And sometimes I've thought, Why not let him? It's the honor of the county is in it, and he's the grand dog, surely. But he isn't mine, after all, and it isn't my business," said John, with a great air of virtue.

"John," I said, "did the boys feel unhappy about it?"

"I wouldn't say yes or no," said John carefully. "But they did mention your dog. They've most of them seen him.

And they all say he's a grand dog and wished George Beirne had had him so he could fight, the way it used to be in the old days."

"John," I said, "I'll let him fight." And when I said that, I knew I had been wanting to all along.

"Will you?" said John.

"Yes."

John grinned and then grew serious. "Mister Teddy," he said. and offered his hand, "you're a credit to the county."

I felt very proud as I shook John's hand, and I looked down at Leonidas with confidence and excitement.

John was practical. "Of course, you can't handle him yourself, and it's no discredit to you either, Mister Teddy. It takes years to make a man handle a dog properly. If you want, though, I'll handle him for you."

"Yes," I said, feeling my ignorance.

"He's in fine shape," said John. "Running the country all summer like the conqueror he is. I've got to go to Boonville on an errand for Miss Kathy, and I'll stop in to the bar and let the boys know. We'll make the arrangements, and I'll tell you tomorrow morning."

"Do you think he'll win, John?" I asked, for it seemed a matter of form to me.

"Sure he will," said John. "I'll be having my own money on him. And so will the boys. But Mister Teddy," he added, "I wouldn't be talking about it. It's you that's doing this for the honor of the county, but there's some wouldn't rightly understand."

"I won't," I said.

But walking home that afternoon with the white dog placidly keeping me company, I asked him if he was afraid and if he minded, and I talked to him as if he understood every word. And perhaps he did. For there was no fear in his walk, and I felt so proud of him that it was on the tip of my tongue twenty times to tell my mother that Leonidas was fighting for Oneida County against the drummer's dog of Loftus Company.

For three days I moved in what seemed a haze of glory. John Callant was making excursions at night and holding rendezvous with all the boys in our valley, and during the daytime one or another would turn up at Uncle Ledyard's stable for a word with John about this, that, or the other, and the fulfillment of the simple errand would require them to step out back with Leonidas while I watched from the stable door, and then they would come in again, and the boy would shake hands with me solemnly and wish me and my dog luck. I felt that the days of youth had passed for me and that I had entered man's estate.

And the only thing that troubled me was the dignity of my dog in letting them feel his muscles or look at his teeth. "He isn't a savage one with people," said John Callant. "He doesn't waste himself with growling. But I tell you he will fight, Adam. Just as a good horse is quiet in the barn."

They would nod and estimate weights and go away, and John Callant would tell me afterward that they had decided to bet this much or that much on my dog. "The boys are all cheering for you, Mister Teddy. You and the fine dog. It's a great thing for them, to be sure." And he made it seem a great thing, in fact.

The wonder of it was that with all the greatness of the fact, no word of it got to my family. It was as if a palisade had been secretly erected around my father's place. Nor did any word of it get to Boyd House, for, as John said, Doone wasn't friendly to the fighting of dogs and he wasn't sure about Uncle Ledyard anymore.

When he said that, my first doubt rose in me, but he smothered it by telling me that George Beirne had been approached and had been agreed on by the drummer and himself as referee. "It isn't just another catch match," said John. "It's a great fight for the world. He's said he'd referee it, and he's coming down this morning to look at the dog."

George Beirne was Uncle Ledyard's cousin. He was almost as tall but more slender, and his features were more finely cut. He looked very handsome walking into the barn in his immaculate muslin driving coat, with his white hat tilted sidewise and his blue eyes shrewdly estimating the dog. As I watched I felt they were of a kind. If George Beirne was in it, I had nothing to worry about.

He passed his hand over the dog's back and down his legs. "He's a magnificent specimen," he said. "Teddy, you're a stouthearted lad." He shook hands, nodded at John, and walked out.

John gazed admiringly after him. "He's one of the real gentry for you, Mister Teddy. Of course, he couldn't wish you luck, being the referee."

Before George Beirne left, he had a word alone with John Callant in the barn. And directly after John came up to me as I sat on the rails of the track and said, sidewise, out of the corner of his mouth, "The fight's tomorrow night."

"Where, John?"

"In Bender's barn, at nine o'clock."

"Bender's?" I asked, for Bender ran a modern dairy on the Boonville road.

"The old barn," said John. "The one back down the cattle lane."

"Oh," I said. "The one with the hole in the roof."

John nodded.

I thought for a moment. "John, how are you going to get Leonidas down?"

"Sure, I'll lead him along the lane, and Adam Fuess's brother'll pick us up by the spring box."

"I'll meet you there," I said.

John's chewing froze in midswing. "You're not coming, surely?"

"I'm coming, John."

"But your mother won't let you out."

"I'll say I'm coming over to Boyd House, or I want to go fishing, or something."

"Sure, and if she finds out, I'll be murdered entirely," said John. "First her and then Mister Ledyard, not to mention Mister Doone."

"I don't care," I said. "I want to be there."

"You'd better be letting me take the dog," said John after a while. "I'm to handle him, anyway."

He had to run off then to take in Maidy, but in a minute he rejoined me while Doone was limbering Arrogance up.

"You can take Leonidas, John," I said after a while.

"It's best," said John.

It was one of those hot nights when the mist lies close to the river bottom and the voices of the old bullfrogs are heavy. As I walked along the river by myself in the dark, the road seemed lonesome to me, and I noticed the shadows of stumps as I had not noticed them for a long time. I missed the white shape of Leonidas that should be walking evenly at my knee. And I was half afraid to go on.

But then I began to think of him standing up for the county against the big-city dog, and I felt that I had to go on. He had looked very dubious as I tied him to the wall ring in the empty box stall, and I had done my best to explain to him. When I looked over the wall a moment later, he was sitting as I had tied him, very still, with his ears pointed and his face to the door through which I had gone. Then he had become aware of me, and his tail had rustled the straw gently. He looked lonely as marble there, and all the way home to my supper I seemed to feel him sitting there looking into the empty blankness above the stall wall. And when at last he heard feet, it would be John Callant's he heard, not mine. John Callant would take him away in the darkness, and I seemed to be able to see him, walking beside John's bowed legs, with his dignity upon him like white armor, unquestioning, affable, and strong with his own courage. The thought of that made me walk on more sturdily. John Callant would handle him right.

Luckily, my mother had gone away to Lyons Falls for dinner that evening, and she would not be back till past midnight. I had nothing to trouble me there, and my whole mind was on the dog.

It was easier walking when I came out of the woods, for there was starlight on the mist and shapes assumed their natural form. I could make out the cows grazing in the night pasture through the mist, the silver wet of dew on their horns, their muzzles glistening. By Hawkinsville I heard a rig rattle over the long bridge and knew that a

wagon was going toward the fight. There were only men's
voices aboard.

And I pressed on through the village, climbing the hill
and crossing the canal at the top of it. A couple of boats
had tied up in front of Amos's. I could see their cabin lights
reflected on the water, and I heard Art Maybe's voice talking to the two boaters. "Yeah," he was saying, "it's little
Teddy Armond's dog. John Callant says he's a dinger, but
I've got my money on the drummer's. It stands to reason,
a dog that wins in seven fights in a row must have the grit
in him."

I never had liked Art Maybe before, and I certainly never
liked him afterward.

"What do you say, Pete?" said one of the boaters. "Might
as well have a look at it."

"Might as well," said the other.

"I'll give you a lift over," said Maybe. I hurried on.

I was afraid. It was the first time it had occurred to me
that there might be any doubt of the result. John Callant
had said the boys all had their money on my dog, yet here
was Art Maybe, notoriously close with cash, putting his
money on the drummer's dog. Perhaps the others were all
betting against Leonidas.

It seemed to me suddenly as if I were alone in the world
and that Leonidas was by himself and we were separated,
and the one thing we both needed was to get a sight of each
other.

I ran for a while. But when a rig rattled up behind me,
instead of hailing it I climbed over the stone wall and lay
down on the far side. A second wagon was overtaking the
first, and the second driver hailed, "Hey, there!"

The first wagon hauled up.

"Where's the fight?"

The driver of the first wagon bawled back, "Bender's barn."

"Whereabouts is that?"

"I guess likely if you follow me you'll come pretty close to it."

The man laughed, and the second driver blew his nose and said, "I've come clear from Port Leyden, and I feared I wasn't going to get there."

"Say, have you seen this drummer's dog fighting?"

"He's a slasher," said the Port Leyden man. "That's his name."

"Well," said the Hawkinsville man, "I've got a dollar on your dog, and I've got another loose in here."

"That's fine," said the Port Leyden man. "It's going to get a lot looser. Not but what I'd like to see that drummer licked. But a man has to make money when he can. Boys, you ain't seen that slasher in action yet, but you're going to see a lot."

He laughed and the men in the first wagon laughed, and one said, "I calculate it'll be a close mix. I ain't seen a real fight since Mr. Beirne was pitting his dogs. But John Callant says that Teddy Armond's dog is all right."

Their voices faded out ahead of me.

I got back into the road and ran. I was afraid then I would be too late. I could see more rigs coming from Boonville, and still more coming from Forestport. I was appalled to think how many rigs there were. I had thought that there would be only a small crowd, but the rigs and the men in them measured like hundreds against the sky. And as I cut across Bender's day pasture, their voices came to me as they talked back and forth, laughing a little loosely. And Art Maybe's wagon with the two boaters in it trailed their hoarse voices in a boating song.

I felt wildly resentful of them all. I began to understand that it didn't mean fighting a dog for the honor of the county at all. For there was whiskey in their voices; the sound of them was like a breath in the night sky, and the shapes of their heads above the hedges made ugly blots against the stars. And I ran with all my might.

Long before I reached Bender's old barn, I saw the lantern light making threads between the warped boards of the walls. Its old, swaybacked roof stood against the sky all alone. And it had the smell of old wood and must and cobwebs, the mingled smell of dry rot in the rafters and the moldy unsunned earth under the rotting cow-stable floor. It was as if the ancient walls had shut in a section of the world's air long ago when the oldest Bender built them, so long ago that the air died there and became like a gray body. The voices of the gathered crowd were heavy against it.

As I stood on the far side of the barn by the old caved-in cellar hold of the first Bender house, I was afraid to go in. It seemed to me that a metamorphosis had taken place with the gathering of those men's voices. And though I could recognize a voice here and there, I was not sure of knowing it, for the tones were rampant with the ease of men in their own company. The horses hitched to the railings of the old barnyard lifted their heads from time to time and pointed their ears toward the barn.

I didn't want to be in among the men now. I was afraid of them. But I couldn't stop myself from going close to the walls. And finally I crept in through the cow door and stood under the mow floor.

Their feet were just over my head, but their voices now sounded far above me, and they echoed with a strange cavernlike quality in the hollow of the roof. I went down the length of the roof. I went down the length of the decaying stanchions until I came to the hay drop, and there I found a series of cleats mounting a studding, ladderlike. I put my hands on one and found it solid, and I began to climb in the dark. I got to the top and found myself at the height of the eaves with the darkness of the roof peak over me and to my left the warm shine of the lanterns making a haze in the moted air. A straw rack ran from my hands out to the edge of the wagon run, and I climbed out on it and crawled along it on my belly, making no noise, until I could look down.

There must have been thirty or forty men clustered around an open space in the middle of the wagon run. The smoke from their pipes mounted lethargically past my face and drifted out into the shadows of the empty mows. The lanterns they carried showed me every detail of their faces, but even the faces I recognized I did not seem to know. Some were eager, some tense with the money involved, some inane from the whiskey, some were openly savage, and one or two were cool and taking stock. But all had a strange masklike quality, as if they had been painted by the lantern light. And their voices were lustful, and as I listened to the bandied estimations of the dogs, and of the bets going one way and another, it seemed to me that I was losing my hold on the world, and that the valley I lived in wasn't the Black River Valley I had always thought it was, but an alien place and I a stranger in it.

For the voices had no meaning in my ears.

And then the crowd parted by the door and George

Beirne walked in. He was cool and neat in his light coat, the lantern shone silver on his white hair, and he greeted the men he knew. He stood in the middle of the floor and examined the footing in the ring.

The wave of voices that had met him died, and men began moving their heads to see out of the door. A man directly under me pulled out a thick silver watch and said, "It's just lacking a minute of nine," and I recognized the watch as Adam Fuess's and felt a brief wonder that I had not recognized him.

Then the men below me seemed to stiffen, the quick, dry sound of their breathing infected me, and I felt my own back grow stiff as I lay on my belly. And the drummer walked in out of the dark. He walked in with the dog short-leashed and shook hands with George Beirne. He was a pasty-skinned man with pinched city clothes and yellow shoes, and his eyes were black and sharp. He had a cigarette stuck to his underlip, and when he talked, the cigarette pointed his words like a small white finger.

His voice was flat. "Any corner suits me, mister. Me and Slasher ain't interested in corners. All we want is a little dog." He grinned thinly around the staring faces, and the cigarette drooped in his face.

He turned around, and I saw the dog. He was a good bull terrier, but he had a tendency to stand out at the elbows too far. He was coarser through the chest than Leonidas, and one of his ears was chewed and torn from an old fight. There were thin welts of scars along his throat. But he faced the door with his feet braced and his good ear cocked, and the black spots on his hide lay dark as ink.

The heads of the men moved this way and that to see him, but he stood quite still, and after a moment we all waited again. We did not hear John Callant arriving. We did not know he had come until the throat of the drummer's dog tippled and his low growl came out of him. Then his hair rose in a slow, short wave over his shoulders, and his feet seemed to plant themselves on the floor, though he hadn't moved at all.

And I saw Leonidas. John Callant had a thong on him, but he walked in beside the little man coolly and stopped on the edge of the ring with the deliberate slowness of perfectly made muscles. A cry rose in my throat and hung in my mouth at the sight of him. He wasn't as heavy as the other dog; he didn't look cocky. But the poised, white perfection of his body was clean as a new sword among those men.

John Callant walked forward to George Beirne and shook hands, and he nodded to the drummer, but the two dogs had forgotten the crowd, and their eyes saw only each other. And the crowd went through its inane moving of heads again. Its words were a hoarse murmuring in my ears, and I didn't hear at all what George Beirne was saying in his cool, clipped speech.

I could see only Leonidas. I saw him back slowly under John's urging until he was opposite the drummer's dog on the other side of the ring. I saw John Callant crouch over him, taking him between his knees. I saw John's hands, with the dirty, scarred nails, moving over his white body and loosening the thong around his neck. And I jumped up on the platform and shouted down on them to stop it.

Their faces turned toward me with a weird slowness, first one and then another and another, until all of them were staring up at me.

"I won't let him fight!" I cried.

I saw John's mouth gaping, and George Beirne came under the platform and looked up at me. He was perfectly cool. "I thought you'd agreed to this, Teddy."

"I did. But I don't want to now."

He said, "But you said you would, Teddy," very quietly. "John Callant told me so."

"I did," I repeated, my voice a dry pain in my throat. "But I don't care. He's my dog."

The drummer looked up from his crouch and his lip sneered. The cigarette was short on his lip now, and he had to squint his eyes against the smoke. "I might have known it," he said in his flat voice. "There ain't anybody here has got a decent dog with guts." He laughed shortly.

A hoarse growl rose out of the men, and one or two I knew stepped out under me and looked up with George Beirne. "Come on, Teddy," they said. "You go home, and we'll look out for things."

"I won't!" I cried.

"You said you'd put him against the slasher," they said.

"He's my dog!" I shouted desperately. "I won't let him!"

Joe Miller stepped up with the others. He was a hand on our own farm. "I'm here, ain't I, Teddy?" he said. "You know me."

"I don't care who's here!" I felt the tears coming out of my eyes, but I couldn't stop them. "He won't fight!" I yelled.

"Look at him," said Joe Miller. "He ain't scared, Teddy." And he pointed a bent hand at Leonidas.

The dog hadn't moved. His head might have dropped a little, but his muzzle was pointed straight at the drummer's dog. And his throat fluttered gently.

"I don't care!" I shouted again, helplessly.

It was like a dream, myself battering against those red faces with my small, repeated words, and the faces rising at me, growing larger in my sight, great boulders of flesh I couldn't stop or even close my eyes against.

Then a man swore and another cried, "Hear that!"

And I heard a rig coming rapidly through the Bender yard and swinging into the cow lane. The horse was a trotter and a fast one. The wheels bucketed over the stony piece and into the old barnyard, and I gave a shout as I saw Uncle Ledyard tramping up the ramp to the mow doors.

He shouldered the men aside until he stood in the middle of the ring beside George Beirne. He paid no attention to the men. He just glanced at the dogs, the drummer, and John, and he looked up at me with his eyes hard and his mouth shut tight in his beard, and he said to George Beirne, "What's going on, George?"

George Beirne said coolly, "A match has been made of Teddy's dog against this drummer's."

"I didn't know, Uncle Ledyard!" I cried.

Uncle Ledyard's face grew dark.

George Beirne said, "He gave permission," and shrugged his shoulders.

Uncle Ledyard turned on John Callant. "Did he?"

"Yes, your honor," said John, with terror all over him.

"Did you, Teddy?" Uncle Ledyard asked me quietly.

"Yes," I blubbered, "but I didn't know how it would be."

"Stop sniveling," Uncle Ledyard said harshly.

Then Doone came in with his face black with passion. He spoke shortly to Uncle Ledyard. "Naturally he didn't," he said. "Probably they've all been working on him. You did, John?"

"Indeed and I didn't," John Callant said indignantly. "Would I be corrupting a lad? I said it was his own dog all the time. Didn't I, Mister Teddy?"

Uncle Ledyard looked up at me again.

"Yes," I said, "but I didn't know."

"George," said Uncle Ledyard, "I think you might have told me about it."

"I was promised to secrecy before I knew which dog it was," said George Beirne. "Besides, what of it, Ledyard?"

"It's a dirty business that no decent man would dirty his hands on," said Uncle Ledyard. "Persuading a child to put his pet up to be slaughtered."

"Slaughtered is it?" cried John Callant. "I'll bet my next month's salary he won't, Mister Ledyard!"

"Be damned to you, John, and keep your mouth shut till I speak to you!" roared Uncle Ledyard.

"Say," said the drummer in his flat voice, "is this a church benefit or a dogfight?"

"You keep quiet, too," said Uncle Ledyard, "if you want to get out of here with your hide whole."

But the crowd were beginning to get up their courage. "How about our money?" they said.

Uncle Ledyard spoke to George Beirne.

"It's the biggest match there's been around here since the old days," said George Beirne. "There's a lot of money outside this crowd, Ledyard."

"Wait a minute then," said Uncle Ledyard. "Teddy, jump down." He held out his thick arms and I jumped and he caught me under the armpits.

"George," he said, "I put you on your honor not to let any fight start for five minutes. Come with me, Teddy."

His big hand fell on my shoulder, and he walked me

outdoors and around the barn out of hearing. He sat down on an old beam and told me to sit beside him. "Teddy," he said, "it's a bad business."

I could hear him breathing deeply beside me. There was something comforting about the familiar scent of him, the strong tobacco smell and the flavor of his clean stables. I felt my nerves slipping, and I tried hard not to cry. "They said it was for the honor of the county, Uncle Ledyard. It sounded fine. But I didn't know."

His breath roughened a moment. Then his thick arm passed over my shoulders. "Teddy," he said quietly, "you ought to have known that if the honor of the county was involved, I'd be in it."

"I didn't think."

"Lots of us don't think, Teddy. It makes us do mean, senseless things. If there was anything worth fighting for, don't you see we'd do the fighting ourselves? We don't ask our friends to go out and knock down a man that needs it, do we? And we don't send our dogs."

"I know."

"But, Teddy, you've said your dog would fight. You've given your word, and, right or wrong, a lot of men have taken it as good. Right or wrong, they've put money—many of them more than they can afford probably—on this fight. I don't like it. I don't like it so much that I'd pay off all the money out of my own pocket if I could. But I think you'd be ashamed if I did that."

I nodded.

"I think, if you want to know, Teddy—"

"Yes," I said.

"I think you've got to put it through. It's the only thing to do now."

I drew in my breath miserably. "All right, Uncle Ledyard."

"And I think you ought to tell them yourself. Tell them you've decided to go through with it, but that, win or lose, it's the last time you'll fight your dog in a match."

"I'm afraid, Uncle Ledyard."

He didn't speak, but put his hand on my shoulder again and pulled me up. We walked slowly up the dark ramp to the lighted door and side by side into the ring. I tried to speak, but I think Uncle Ledyard relented when he looked at me.

"Gentlemen," he said, "Mr. Armond has asked me to say to you that he has decided to let his dog fight, but win or lose he'll not fight him again."

They cheered. They weren't cheering his speech. They were yelling for the fight they had been waiting for.

Uncle Ledyard leaned over me. "Do you want to stay, Teddy?"

I felt sick, but his hand on my shoulder gave me a kind of courage and I nodded.

"Good lad," he said, and drew me back to the edge of the ring. Doone came over to my other side and put his hand on my other shoulder. I stood between them staring straight across the ring at Leonidas. There was a buzzing in my ears so that I didn't hear, and my eyes could not clearly follow what happened.

All I saw was his white shape walking out slowly from John's hands. Stiff-legged, he looked, as if he were walking on his toes, and his head was high.

And then his head dropped, and I saw the muscles swelling behind his ears, and his lip lifted from his teeth. There was a deep snarling, and I turned my eyes to see the other dog charge. He was more like a bull than a dog, with his overheavy chest and his crooked forelegs and his torn ear drooping like a broken horn. He came like a shot, and behind him I saw the drummer still crouched, his mouth a little open to show one gold front tooth, his hands spread.

It was a trick some dogs learn, John told me afterward, for fighting inexperienced dogs, using the shoulder and his weight to knock the other off balance. And John held his breath, for a fight could be lost right there.

But I did not know that. All I saw was the savagery in the drummer's dog—the tips of froth along his lips and his strong teeth. And it seemed to me that Leonidas would be knocked over. I did not see how he turned, but his tail lifted like a sword, and when the drummer's dog whirled with claws rasping on the old plank floor, Leonidas was facing him and in the same instant sprang. It seemed to me he fought cleanly and honestly, without tricks and without feinting. That time he missed his strike on the drummer's dog's throat, but his teeth caught just before the shoulder and a thin ribbon of red slashed the other's white front. And the drummer's dog's teeth clicked sharply as he missed the hold he had expected.

And then they moved so fast my eyes could not follow them but saw them in quick poses, held for an infinitesimal space in time and lost again in the fluid interchange of posture. I saw the head of Leonidas come up, the ears clean and white and flat against his neck, a red streak against his shoulder and a gray patch of slaver on his back. And I saw him go down before a sudden charge, and the flash of his feet as he kicked himself free and came up under a second charge, looking white hot and a yellow fire in his eyes. He made no sound, though the drummer's dog had clipped his flank. But the drummer's dog snarled, like a dog singing to himself, and the men behind pushed against us and shouted.

But the drummer's dog was panting as he sprang again, and I felt sick. My eyes swung desperately away around the men's faces, and they were blurred red spots I could not see. I closed my eyes and prayed I would not shame Uncle Ledyard and Doone by being sick.

And I heard a sudden, desperate clutching of toenails in the rough boards and the sudden letting out of breath from the men's throats, and then a great shout; I opened my eyes and saw the drummer's dog rolling free, a great slash on him, and Leonidas was standing with his head down and his lips red. I saw his loins gather as he sprang and their jaws clashed teeth to teeth like the meeting of bucks' horns, and I looked around again.

I saw the drummer still crouching, with his eyes like slits and his mouth unsneering. And I saw George Beirne tense, with a kind of fire in his eyes and a sadness, too, as if in his breast he felt the breath of long-lost times. And I saw John Callant squatting on his hams, his mouth grinning like a frog's.

I turned again to the dogs with my heart feeling bigger than my chest, and I saw Leonidas poised again. His tail was up and his ears flat, and he sprang once more.

The drummer's dog went down.

They made no sound now, for Leonidas had found the hold and he had the throat. The other dog kicked under him. But Leonidas's muscles made a hump in front of his shoulders, and he bore him back.

George Beirne moved over to the drummer. "He's beaten."

The drummer cursed. "No, he ain't."

"He's beaten," said George Beirne. "He made a good fight."

"He's gone under," said the drummer. There was a strange kind of agony on his pasty face. "Let him lay."

"I'm going to break them," said George Beirne.

"For God's sake then," said the drummer, and his knees trembled as he rose.

I did not see any more. I heard them sloshing water over the dogs, and then Uncle Ledyard had me by the shoulder, and he marched me out of the barn. I looked back once, and Doone was coming behind me. He had Leonidas on leash, and the dog made a pale, fine marble at his side. He was walking quietly, and his dignity was on him.

When Uncle Ledyard boosted me into the rig, I was crying. I did not dare to look at Leonidas as Doone lifted him in beside me. I did not help him up on the seat. I only dimly felt the lurch of the wagon as Uncle Ledyard climbed on and then Doone. They sat together on the front seat, and Doone turned Arrogance into the lane.

Leonidas got up on the seat beside me and lay down. His head was bent to lick the slash in his flank. He licked it quietly with his eyes closed.

Uncle Ledyard and Doone were silent.

I looked at Leonidas, as he was not looking at me, and dared not touch him. And then he lifted his head to sniff the air running past us and put his head to my hand and licked it.